JEWELLED EYE

Also by Douglas Clark:

THE BIG GROUSE
PLAIN SAILING
STORM CENTER

JEWELLED EYE

EYE

DOUGLAS CLARK

PERENNIAL LIBRARY

Harper & Row, Publishers, New York
Cambridge, Philadelphia, San Francisco, Washington
London, Mexico City, São Paulo, Singapore, Sydney

A hardcover edition of this book was published in Great Britain in 1985 by Victor Gollancz Ltd. It is here reprinted by arrangement with John Farquharson, Ltd.

First PERENNIAL LIBRARY edition published 1988.

Library of Congress Cataloging-in-Publication Data

Clark, Douglas.
  Jewelled eye.

  Originally published: London : V. Gollancz, 1985. I. Title.
PR6053.L294J4   1988   823'.914   87-46130
ISBN 0-06-080919-1 (pbk.)

88 89 90 91 92 OPM 10 9 8 7 6 5 4 3 2 1

JEWELLED
EYE

1

Detective Chief Superintendent George Masters leant into the wind as he made his way along the open promenade of Yourhead. The south-westerly gale blowing up the Bristol Channel, unimpeded in its long journey from mid-Atlantic, was enough to cause him to gasp with the effort of making headway against it. He was alone on the long grey stretch of concrete. The grass and flowerbeds to his left shone greasily under the yellow light of the wide-spaced lamps. The road beyond that was deserted black tarmac with occasional glimpses of white and yellow lines on its surface. In the small cottages bordering the road, not a light was to be seen. He guessed the occupants had locked up for the night, retreating to back rooms to escape the draughts which would seek out and whistle through the smallest gaps round front windows and doors.

The tide was breaking white over the rocks on the beach and—where it had managed to get in as far as the promenade wall—was flinging spray up in showers over the pathway he was walking. He tried to avoid the worst of them, but they came without warning. The howl of the wind drowned the thresh of the sea, but somewhere a signboard swinging wildly on rusty hinges was producing a high-pitched squeal that was audible above the gale.

One of the thatched cottages, he had been told. The first few were slate-roofed. Nearer the tiny harbour, among the older ones, would be the one he sought. He crossed over the grass and then the road to a pavement hardly wide enough for one person to walk on. He noted that all the doors, opening on to the pavement, were lower than the flagstones and each had wooden slots at the bottom of the door jambs. Into these, in all cases, had been inserted storm boards to stop the worst of any flooding should the tide come over the promenade.

Thirty-five. It had the number painted on a tile let into the plaster of the front wall. And a name, too, painted black on an oval section of wood, cut from some tree trunk and then varnished over. He had to peer hard to read it. "Driftwood." He wondered about that name for a moment. The board was newish. Had Gudgeon christened this house afresh? He thought not. It wouldn't be in character. Gudgeon wouldn't be mawkish, ever.

There was a bell-pull. Masters took it and used it gently. It looked as if firm treatment would bring it off its fixings. He felt momentarily pleased to hear the sound of the bell. He judged it to be immediately inside the house.

There followed a longish wait before he heard movement. Then, after the sound of bolts being drawn, the top half of the door opened. Inside, a man struggled to prevent it crashing back under the force of the wind.

"Who the devil's that?"

"Major Gudgeon?"

"Of course I'm Gudgeon. Who the hell . . . good God, it's Masters, isn't it?"

"That's right."

"I don't know what you want, but you'd better come in. I can't have the gale blowing the place away." The top half of the door was closed again and bolted to the lower half before Gudgeon opened the whole.

"Step over the board—and watch yourself. The floor's half a foot lower than the pavement."

Masters did as he had been instructed and then leant his weight to help close the door.

"This way."

Gudgeon led on, out of the little hall with its varnished wooden walls and into a living-room. Masters saw that he had been mistaken about the residents retreating to the back-quarters. This room went from front to back of the cottage. Behind the incompletely closed curtain he could see the window had been covered by internal shutters, allowing no light to escape to the outside.

"You're the last person I ever expected to see as a guest in this house." They regarded each other for a moment. "But perhaps you don't come as a guest? Of course you don't. What would a senior detective from Scotland Yard be doing down here, hundreds of miles from his own ground, in weather like this, if it wasn't a duty trip?"

Masters, still wearing his topcoat with the collar turned up, continued to gaze at Gudgeon. The ex-soldier was squat in comparison with himself. Five feet ten or so, with broad shoulders and a powerful, muscular body. The head was well shaped, the features handsome, if a trifle heavy. He was dressed in neatly pressed grey slacks and a navy-blue, roll-necked fisherman's jersey. The shoes on his feet were old slip-ons, obviously battered, and yet clean and highly polished. "I am on a duty trip," admitted Masters. "But this visit is not part of that trip. It is just a visit."

Gudgeon grinned sardonically. "On such a night as this?"

"Happening to find myself in the area. . . ."

"If we're going to quote bromides at each other, you've wasted your time."

"I was hoping I hadn't."

"Obviously, otherwise you wouldn't have come."

"No."

"Take your coat off."

Masters accepted the invitation. The room was too invitingly cosy for standing around in a greatcoat. The stone fireplace had a wood fire on the hearth. Great pieces of grey timber blazing with the yellow sodium flame that showed they had at some time been soaked in salt water. Jetsam, thrown up on the beach by the tides and presumably collected by Gudgeon virtually out-

3

side his own front door. And under the blazing timbers a great mound of wood ash, blushing red-hot with every movement of the air in the chimney and then assuming a thin grey coating of spent material as crisp and crumbly as the outside of a rice cake. On both sides of the hearth an armchair, a real armchair in hide, with between the two a footstool big enough to be used by both sides at once. And a circular dining-table with bits and pieces on it to show the room was lived in. A bookcase crammed with well-used volumes. A cabinet, presumably for drinks. A glass-fronted china cupboard. Several decent prints. And a low ceiling to give an atmosphere of yellow-lighted cosiness.

As Gudgeon took Masters' coat and placed it on a wheel-back chair at the table, he said: "I don't have to ask how you found me. I suppose you've kept a check on some damned police computer."

"Not a bit of it."

"Then how?"

"I didn't know where you were hanging out until earlier today, after I arrived in Yourhead."

"And you suddenly discover I'm here, just like that? Who d'you think you're fooling, Masters? How could you possibly arrive in a town the size of Yourhead and just discover that I live here unless you had asked questions concerning me? Which in turn means that you knew I was here. And that gives the lie to your story."

"Not a bit of it. Supports it, rather."

Gudgeon gestured to Masters to take one of the fireside chairs and himself took the one opposite.

"I have asked questions in Yourhead," agreed Masters, "but none concerning you."

"But my name just happened to crop up."

"Not quite. I never mentioned your name to anybody and, quite truly, I did not know until you opened your front door to me that you were the Gudgeon I knew."

The Major started to fill a pipe. Masters followed his example. He had rubbed the Warlock Flake ready for the bowl before he gave any further explanation.

4

"Your name appeared in a list I had asked my sergeants to get for me."

"All the old lags living in the area?"

"Nothing like that. I asked for a list of names of the people who live in these cottages at the harbour end of the sea front. After I got it, I saw your name. C. R. Gudgeon, with a note beside it."

"Saying what?"

"'Lives alone. Believed to be a retired military man.'"

Gudgeon laughed aloud. "Just that? Like that?"

"Exactly like that." Masters leant forward to use one of the twisted paper tapers that stood in a container on the hearth. He lit it at the fire and applied it to his pipe. Gudgeon watched him carefully, with the interest of one devotee in how another manages.

"That raises a couple of points," said Gudgeon at last.

"I'm sure you think so."

"What business brought you to Yourhead in the first place, and having got here, why the interest in Excise Row?"

"I thought one of your two questions would be to ask why I came to visit you simply because I'd seen and recognized your name."

"Oh, I know the answer to that one. You want something from me."

"You seem very sure of that."

"Come off it, Masters. Altruistic motives from a copper—no matter how exalted—on a night like this? If there'd been a wind as strong as this on the first Christmas night, the Archangel Gabriel wouldn't have paid his visit. He'd have put it off for a day or two."

Masters took his pipe from his mouth and appeared to consider it appreciatively for a few moments. Then: "How can you possibly suppose there can be something I want from you? Unless, of course, there is something you think I ought to know about and which you haven't yet reported to the police?"

"There's nothing. Why should there be?"

"There we are then. If there's nothing, there can be

5

no reason—other than an altruistic one—for my visit."

"You honestly mean to say you came here because of my bonny blue eyes?"

"Not quite. I felt I would like to look you up."

"For old times' sake?"

"That's about it."

"But you are still here on duty and, willy-nilly, my name has cropped up in your investigations. At least I take it you are investigating something?"

Masters nodded. "It would be idle to pretend I came down here for fun at this time of the year."

Gudgeon got to his feet and took a litre of whisky and two glasses from the cabinet. Without asking whether Masters would like a drink, he poured two large tots and handed one to his visitor.

"Thank you. Good health."

"Cheers."

After a moment, Gudgeon set his heavy-based glass down firmly on the corner of the hearth. "Well?" he asked. "Is that it?"

"More or less. I thought—no, I didn't think, the idea just occurred to me—that you were so near to the hotel where I am staying, it would be churlish not to call on you."

"Do you call on all the ex-cons you've arrested?"

"I've met the odd one from time to time," confessed Masters.

"Why?"

"I don't understand the question."

"What emotion causes you to want to see them? Regret? A desire to gloat? A wish for forgiveness, perhaps?"

Masters grimaced. "Nothing of that sort. If my job affected me in that way, I wouldn't do it. I'd become a tax-collector or something equally lovable."

Gudgeon took up his glass again. The atmosphere in the room was pleasant and cosy. A good fire, comfortable chairs, a drink, books and papers lying about without

6

any hint of squalor, and to enhance it all, the dark and blustery night outside, kept at bay by this stout little house.

Masters looked about him appreciatively. "How long have you been here?"

"Just over two years."

"Ever since. . . ?"

"Ever since they let me out. With full remission for good behaviour, of course."

"Snug in winter, delightful in summer?"

"Precisely. A cushy billet."

"And you live entirely alone? By that I mean you look after yourself?"

Gudgeon grinned. "If you're prying into my sex-life, I can assure you no woman has slept under this roof since I moved in."

"I was not prying into your affairs. I am so struck by the obvious care lavished on your home that I thought I detected a woman's hand."

"Detected? It's obvious. In an isolated place like Your-head, which lives off holiday-makers, there are plenty of women who have been employed in housework of one sort or another all their lives. In hotels, boarding-houses and the like. Now that their trade has taken a knock and, places have closed down, they're willing to come and look after people like me. I have a Mrs Shaw. I'd like to be able to say she is a jewel."

"But she isn't?"

"Shall we say a jewel slightly flawed. Not of the first water, perhaps. But she's amiable and godly clean. Her trouble is that things go wrong on her. All electric appliances cease to function very soon after she switches them on. For instance, though I have a Hoover, she uses a hand-propelled sweeper on this carpet most days. When she isn't here on a Sunday I go over it with the electric job."

"But otherwise?"

"I've got a gas cooker. A modern one. The spark ig-

7

niter—which is electric—no longer works for her, but she manages with a box of matches and the results are good, if plain."

"You look fit and well fed."

"Did you imagine I would have gone to pieces?"

"Some men would."

"I'm forty. Hardly decrepit."

"Physically, no. But mentally? You had a few knocks. They could have affected you."

"Is that how you describe receiving an unmerited gaol sentence and losing a lovely wife because of it? A few knocks?" Gudgeon got to this feet. "Is that all you came for? Or are you now going to give me the real reason? If so, you can have another drink."

"And if not, I suppose you'd prefer me to go?"

"You can hardly expect me to regard you as my favourite visitor."

"No."

"But you're here for some good reason." He held up a hand to stop any interruption Masters might make. "If it doesn't concern me, as you insist, whom does it concern? You're a murder man mostly. Particularly when you're operating outside the Metropolitan Police area. But I've heard of no murder round here. We're a small town of twenty thousand or so, miles from anywhere. The nearest railway station is an hour's journey away by bus. . . ."

"Taunton?"

Gudgeon nodded. "We're not a hotbed of crime. A few yobs in summer cause a bit of trouble occasionally, but after that it's nothing more than parking fines, and you don't bother your head about those." He held out his hand for Masters' glass. "And as far as I know, I'm the only ex-con in the town."

"That's unlikely. But hasn't it occurred to you that real villains—as opposed to people like yourself who have seen the inside of a gaol for other reasons—might just decide to operate in a nice, isolated-but-not-too-small community like this?"

"A totally unsuspecting community, you mean?"

Masters nodded and accepted the proffered glass.

Gudgeon frowned. "I don't like the idea of some of the types I met inside operating round here. Quite a lot of them would be harmless enough, of course, but others. . . ." He looked hard at Masters as he sat down. "I doubt if even experienced policemen like yourself realize what scum they are. Dangerous scum."

Masters shrugged. "We meet them daily."

"In small doses. And as people having authority. You don't have to rub shoulders with them for months on end on the same level."

"I must admit that is a thought which hadn't struck me before. We see the results of their handiwork, and that often sickens us, but after we've run them in, well, we thank heaven they're banged-up where we don't have to be in their company."

Gudgeon sipped his whisky before saying: "So that's why you're here. Some of the heavy mob have invaded us."

"That's not what I said. To the best of my knowledge there are no villains actually down here. The climate wouldn't suit them and Yourhead doesn't offer. They want the Smoke as much as some nasties need stones to crawl under."

"Flying visits, then?"

"I think, perhaps, some of them have been this way."

"Who? Anybody I might recognize?"

Masters didn't give a direct answer. Instead, he said: "That's why I asked you how long you'd been living here."

"In case I'd recognized anybody whose name and form I might know?"

"Not quite that. What I'm asking is, would you recognize a villain, a man who had been inside—not necessarily with you, but in any of the hard nicks—if you were to see one?"

"Just like that?"

"Yes. I'm talking of hard cases, of course. Not the chap who gets sent down for non-violent crimes."

"Now you're asking."

"I know it's a tall order, almost impossible perhaps, but all the same, would you be able to?"

"I might try, and then find I was wrong four times out of five."

"What would be the average citizen's figures?"

"I think I'd have the slight edge. Say nine times out of ten for the average bloke. But I could be way out in my guesses."

"And your local Yourhead bobby on the beat or in his Panda car?"

"Most of 'em will never have seen a real villain except in TV shows."

"That would be my guess, too."

"Look here, Masters, you've told me you called on me for no reason other than to see me. It now sounds as if you had a motive for your visit."

Masters shook his head. "No motive. What I've spoken about is simply to let you know that I'm down here because a trail I'm following has led me this way. In other words, I think that there might be some connection between this place and a certain amount of long-term skullduggery we've only recently got on to. For reasons we won't go into now, I suspect the area of the harbour here to be involved. That means that villains may come this way. Could even have some sort of safe-house near here. So I asked for the names of the occupants of these houses."

"And found an ex-con was living in one of them. Is that it? You called here to reassure yourself I wasn't one of the villains you're after."

"I never gave that aspect a thought."

"Pull the other one, Masters."

"I came, if I came with any specific object in view, to warn you that there could be the odd nasty character about. Villains you might even know and who might recognize you, or men you might reckon to be villains. I merely wanted you to be on your guard."

"Why?"

"Because if it were to get known on the grapevine that an ex-prisoner like yourself was living here, right on the site of operations, they might decide that your cottage would be a good place for lying low. They could force themselves on you."

"They might try," said Gudgeon grimly.

"If they wanted to, they would succeed," said Masters quietly. "I know you're a trained fighting man, but they are gorillas and they never work alone. You'll have to recognize that there are such things as overwhelming odds."

Gudgeon stared at Masters in surprise. "You said that last sentence as though you're certain some such eventuality will arise. Not could or might. Not conditional."

"I was probably overstating my case, but I put it as strongly as that because I think the chances of it's happening are great."

"Clairvoyant now, are we?"

"Logical. I know some real villains have tramped along the path outside your door in the not-too-distant past. Know that for a fact. I suspect very strongly that they could be repeating the exercise in the not-too-distant future. Now, you must know as well as I do that when such men are on the job, they keep their eyes skinned. And they gather information. I suspect that you walk along the front here, hang about the quayside, and on fine days leave the top half of your front door open?"

"Quite right, I do."

"Villains like looking in through other people's front doors. What if one who could recognize you looked through yours one day and saw you hoovering the carpet in the hall?"

"It's unlikely that any of your villains would know me."

"That I will accept. But if what I think is correct, those boyos will have done as I did and checked who lives in these houses. Not only their names, either, though I suspect the name Major Gudgeon—which may not ring any

11

bells in Yourhead—will be known to every rogue in London. Dammit, man, you killed one of them. They remember such things."

Gudgeon remained silent for a moment or two. Then he said: "I'll admit there could be something in what you say. Thanks for the warning. I'll keep my eyes skinned."

"Please do."

"Meaning that if I see anybody I think might be a villain I inform the local police?"

Masters shook his head. "I think not. One can't arrest even villains unless they are involved in villainy. Walking along the Yourhead front is, on the face of it, an innocuous exercise. The locals could do nothing unless you were actually to report some criminal activity taking place on their patch. And a mere enquiry by them could cause us a lot of trouble by warning these people that we are aware of their presence."

"Us?"

"This is a co-ordinated investigation."

"Ah!"

Masters smiled. "You seem to be aware of the term."

"I read my papers. Not long ago there was an announcement that the Home Secretary had ordered the formation of crime-busting teams for investigating major linked crimes that crossed over interforce boundaries."

Masters nodded.

"Wasn't it as a result of the enquiry by some big bug into the handling—or mishandling—of the Yorkshire Ripper case?"

"Quite right. It was the outcome of a report by the Chief Inspector of Constabulary."

Gudgeon lay back in his chair. "I remember it pretty well, actually, because I thought it was such a good idea. One which should have been brought in years ago. Wasn't there something about cases where Chief Constables couldn't agree on who should be appointed senior investigating officer being referred to the Chief Inspector of Constabulary for a decision?"

"Quite right."

"Then you must be feeling pretty pleased with yourself, Masters, because, as I recall, the report said something about the best detective and forensic science talent in the country being brought to bear on these investigations."

"Something of the sort," admitted Masters.

"And you are in overall charge, I take it?"

"Yes."

"Intent on keeping the locals out."

"Intent on doing a good job. I think the interference of the local bobby on this beat could snarl things up."

"And could be dangerous for him personally, perhaps?"

"That would be a distinct possibility were he to interfere with the men I have in mind."

"Who are they?"

"That is something I can't tell you. Meaning won't."

Gudgeon grinned. "Am I really cabbage-looking, Masters?"

"Far from it."

"You've been burbling on about villains picking me out. Okay, I'll accept that. But I suspect you would not have been so insistent had you not thought there was a good chance of somebody recognizing me or of me recognizing him. Which means, in my book, that at least one of the people you are after was in jug with me. Correct?"

"Really and truly I cannot answer that because I don't know who was in gaol with you. I don't keep track of that sort of thing."

"I'll take your word for it, but I'll bet some computer somewhere is looking into the matter at this very moment and churning out some facts and figures for you."

"We certainly have the use of a computer."

"As I thought."

Masters got to his feet. "I'll call on you again if I may."

"For what reason?"

"To talk to you about one or two things that have happened round here and which you may know of."

"After the computer has put me in the clear?"

"Be your age, Major. If I'd had any doubts on that score do you think I'd have come here at all?"

"You've told me nothing."

"I've partially shown you my hand. Now, I'll have my coat, please. I promised to be back at the hotel in time to have a nightcap with my colleagues."

"How many of you?"

"Four."

"Is that sergeant of yours there? Reed, is it?"

"He's there, together with DCI Green and DS Berger. My usual team, in fact, when I'm away from home and on a big case."

DCI Green, with Sergeants Reed and Berger in neighbouring armchairs, was sprawled on a settee in the lounge of the Water's Edge Hotel. He was reading a colour supplement, the other two were combining in attempting *The Times* crossword.

Green put the magazine down.

"I wonder if there's any of that coffee left?"

"No," replied Berger. "Your sixth cup emptied the pot, so I switched the hotplate off, and before you ask if there are any after-dinner mints left, the answer is no."

"There were two left when. . ."

"I ate them," said Berger. "In an effort to stop you making a pig of yourself."

The Water's Edge was Yourhead's biggest hotel, one of the few that kept open all year. Now, in mid-February, the number of guests was small. Only four tables were occupied in the dining-room at dinner time, so the total was probably no more than twenty. But the residents' bar, lying between the dining-room and the lounge, had been opened promptly at half-past five, which suited Green; and after dinner several large coffee-pots had been left on a hotplate just outside the lounge door, and beside them a full plate of chocolate mints. This arrangement had also suited Green who, when it became obvious that none of the other guests was proposing to stay in the lounge after coffee, had made certain that full use was made of the facilities.

"No more Freeman's?" he complained. "In that case I'll have to have a drink. Which of you two is going to fetch. . . ?"

"Ring the bell," interrupted Reed. "It's on the wall behind you."

The young bartender came in, looking as if he had been asleep for the last hour. Green ordered three beers. The youth brought them and then asked if there would be anything else that evening.

"What's up, son? It's not ten o'clock yet."

"No, sir, but as there hasn't been anybody in the residents' bar since dinner. . . ."

"Want to get to your bed, son?"

"It's not that, sir. They're rather busy through in the public bar. I could go and help."

"Rather busy?" asked Reed. "On a night like this?"

"It's a bad night," replied the youth, "but not all that unusual for winter round here. And the regulars come out, sir. Particularly in cars."

"In that case, son," said Green, "can you leave us a tray? We're expecting Mr Masters back and he'll want a drink."

"What shall I put on it, sir?"

"Eight more bottles. That'll be two apiece. And don't forget a clean glass for the Chief Superintendent and an opener for the bottles."

"Right, sir. Thank you."

The young man brought the tray in.

"Just one thing before you go, son."

"Yes, sir?"

"Will you be waiting in the dining-room at breakfast time?"

"No, sir. Not tomorrow."

"Pity. I wanted to make sure I'd be able to get some fried spud with my bacon and eggs and suchlike."

The youth grinned. "No trouble, sir. Just ask for the

15

Victorian breakfast and you'll get the lot—including potato."

"Thanks, lad. Goodnight, and don't work too hard."

They watched the young man leave. Green sat up to drink and to pass round cigarettes.

"The Chief's taking longer than I thought he would, just to walk down the road and make his number," said Berger.

"He doesn't need a nursemaid," growled Green. "He's a big boy now."

"In that case, why have you looked at your watch a dozen times in the last twenty minutes?"

"I wanted to be sure I got an order in before closing time," replied Green.

"Rubbish. You could have called for that tray at any time, and as a resident here you can get a drink whenever you like, if there's somebody about to serve you."

"Give him another quarter of an hour," said Green, changing tack and thereby disclosing his own disquiet.

"What then? A search party?"

"If a couple of coppers go out for a breath of fresh air of an evening," said Reed, "not even the Chief could regard it as a search party."

"Good try, lad," said Green. "But nobody goes out for a breath of fresh air on a night like this. His nibs would know the score. So we'll give him another quarter."

Berger put his tankard down. "This bloke the Chief's gone to see," he said.

"Gudgeon?"

"Who is he and what is he, and why are we getting all uptight about a chap who can look after himself as well as George Masters can?"

"Don't know anything about him," replied Green, "except that he's an ex-con. And you heard what his nibs said."

"That Gudgeon had killed two men in two separate incidents?"

"Just that, lad. And when jacks go visiting killers on

16

their tod and don't get back when they should, their mates begin to wonder why."

"So you know nothing about this Gudgeon chap?"

"Nothing, except that his nibs sent him down. It was a case I wasn't involved in."

"I was," said Reed. "You were on holiday at the time, and it was before Sergeant Berger joined us."

"So what do you know, lad?"

"I'd have said the Chief would not be in any danger. I know quite a lot about Gudgeon. I didn't realize you two were in the dark."

"You'll be in the dark, lad, unless you tell us quick."

"Why didn't the Chief tell you himself?"

"Because," said Green quietly, "the subject never came up until he looked at that copy of the electoral register Sarn't Berger made at the library. All his nibs asked for was the names of the people occupying those cottages along the esplanade from the point where it stops being a promenade and becomes the roadway leading along to the quay. About a couple of dozen of 'em at most. Any rate, few enough for our friend here to copy out in the time it took me to buy a postcard for my missus in the shop next door."

"Twenty-nine actually," said Berger, "and that included a couple of small shops, the pub at the end of the quay and a small café. I gave the list to the Chief when we met in the bar before dinner. He put it in his pocket without looking at it. But as you know, he didn't have anything off the sweet trolley, and so, while we were eating and he wasn't, he took it out and looked at it. Then all he said was that he'd recognized a name. This chap called C. R. Gudgeon, an ex-con who'd been responsible for a couple of killings. With that he excused himself from the table and went up for his coat. When he came down he said he was off to pay this Gudgeon a visit, that he wouldn't be away that long and he'd have a nightcap with us when he got back."

"What's the matter with you, lad?" Green asked Reed.

17

"Why ask us why his nibs didn't tell us about Gudgeon? It's on a par with everything about this case. There's so much secrecy about it that for all I know we're on our summer holidays, or I'd think so if it wasn't for the weather."

"Sorry," said Reed. "That's what was making me cagey. The secrecy. I thought if the Chief had wanted you to know about Gudgeon, he'd have told you."

"Look, lad," growled Green, "if Gudgeon's an ex-con, his record's an open book for anybody to read. There's no secrecy about it. I could pick up the phone in my room, call the Yard, and have it from CRO inside five minutes. Any of us could."

Reed nodded his agreement with the logic behind this statement.

"So open up," went on Green. "Who's this Gudgeon?"

Reed frowned to concentrate his memory. "I'll try to tell it to you in chronological order. Mark you, the Chief and I weren't concerned in the first case, but we went into it in detail when the second business came up."

"As one always does go into past records," said Green sarcastically.

"To a greater extent than that. We got all the reports and the transcript and . . ."

"So you know it all. Get on with it."

"Gudgeon was a company commander in the army. A major. A young one, and all his annual reports said he was good. His battalion went to Ireland, but just before it went there it got a new colonel and I got the impression he and Gudgeon didn't exactly hit it off."

"It often happens," said Green.

"Gudgeon apparently believed in going out on patrol with his men. Liked to see what they were up against and didn't want them to do what he didn't have to do himself. The Colonel didn't like this and told Gudgeon he should stick with his company HQ in the report centre.

"After a bit, things began to get restless over there.

18

Evidently there are periods of comparative calm and then the muttering starts and everybody knows something big is brewing.

"The Colonel was told he had to try and forestall whatever was coming by making a concentrated sweep one evening. His whole battalion was split up into the usual armed patrols, the police were co-operating, and each patrol was given a definite area to move in. Those areas came from the Colonel himself. He'd worked them out and hadn't left it to company commanders.

"Gudgeon decided he'd go with one of his own groups. The one on the right of his company. He'd got the written orders for his patrol. They were to operate from Street A to Street B."

"In between them?" asked Berger. "All the alleys and side-streets and things?"

"That's right. Anyway, off went Gudgeon with his party, and the draw was pretty tame for about an hour. And then, just as it was getting dusk, but still light enough to see quite a lot, some shots were fired at the patrol when they were in Street B. Only just in it, apparently; at the end and looking along it. One of the lads was hit. While his mates dragged him under cover, Gudgeon took on the gunman. He wasn't too far away. Gudgeon, apparently, could just make him out, though he had the gun flashes to help him as well. The man was standing on the doorstep of a house that opened straight on to the pavement, and so was half hidden by the brickwork of the doorway."

"But Gudgeon got him, did he?" demanded Green.

"First shot," replied Reed. "He shot to kill and he killed him."

"So what happened?"

"There was a hell of a to-do. The gunman was a lad of sixteen. When Gudgeon and his boys got up to him a few minutes later, there was the body on the pavement and no gun to be found. You can imagine what was said. Innocent youth killed by army officer, and all that sort

19

of thing. The news showed his brother saying the lad was simply knocking at the door of the house to be let in. He hadn't been doing any shooting."

"The usual rubbish, in fact."

"Right. Fortunately, the forensic experts could tell from tests on the lad's hands that he had been firing a weapon shortly before they got to the body, and there was the wounded soldier as proof and the policeman with the patrol as witness. So Gudgeon was cleared by the police enquiry. Apparently, taking the gun and leaving the dead body is an old trick the IRA people always try on."

"They just opened the door, reached out for the rifle and left the lad lying there?" asked Berger, scandalized.

"And whipped the weapon away out of the back door before the house could be searched," added Green. He turned to Reed. "So that was one of Gudgeon's killings, was it? But you say he got off."

"He was exonerated by the police enquiry, but his colonel charged him with disobeying orders, thereby putting his men's lives at risk."

"He what? How could he do that?"

"His written orders had said from Street A as far as Street B. The Colonel said Gudgeon should not have been in that street, which his orders had specifically excluded because it was something of a no-go area."

"Specifically?"

"That's what the Colonel was adamant his orders implied. And as an additional charge he stated he had given Gudgeon verbal orders to remain in his report centre."

"The army couldn't get away with that one," said Green. "And it wouldn't want to."

"The army, as such, didn't want to. But if a CO charges one of his officers and remands him for a court martial, there's little anybody can do except dismiss the case when it comes up."

"Whose leg are you pulling?" asked Green. "If the top brass and Judge Advocate's branch don't think the charge should be brought, they can say so, and it's a brave colonel who flouts a general."

"Bureaucrats," said Reed.

"Meaning what?"

"Meaning there was such a hell of a manufactured public outcry against an officer getting away with a killing when some private soldiers have to stand trial for shooting people in Northern Ireland, that the bureaucrats in the Defence Ministry insisted Gudgeon should be tried too. They couldn't get him for murder in a civilian court, because the police had exonerated him, so they got him for disobeying orders in a court martial."

"What happened?"

"I don't know much about the army, so I didn't really understand the defence. But Gudgeon got a QC to defend him. . . ."

"Which he's perfectly entitled to do."

"A chap of about your age who'd served in the infantry during the war—as an officer."

"What happened?"

"He got the Colonel into the box . . ."

"Witness stand."

"Whatever. Then the QC asked if the CO had attended Staff College, which he said he had. 'In that case,' said counsel, 'you'll be familiar with the army publication called *Staff Duties in the Field.*'

"Course the Colonel said he was. So the QC said what orders did that book lay down for officers of whatever rank, generals, brigadiers, colonels, majors, captains or subalterns, when they were given an area of operations either in defence or attack, static role or mobile, for the particular formation they were commanding? The Colonel said the troops were not at war in Northern Ireland. Counsel said that was immaterial. *Staff Duties in the Field* did not specify that the orders were for wartime operations only. It was the Bible for both peace and war, so would the Colonel kindly give him the text book answer to his question."

21

"Clever," said Green. "I remember that bit now. All formations when given orders for occupying country, automatically cover the stated boundary on the right of their area. In other words, that boundary becomes inclusive, whether it's a road, river, railway line, belt of trees or whatever. Always on the right, so that there can never be any mistake and no joining line between two formations is ever left undefended. If the Colonel had wanted Gudgeon not to operate in Street B, he would have had specifically to say that that street was excluded, because 'as far as' in this context means 'as far as and including'."

Reed nodded. "You know more about these things than I do, being an old sweat. But what you've just said was Gudgeon's defence against the charge of disobeying the order about not operating in Street B. On the other business, the one concerned with the Colonel's warning that he should remain with Company HQ at such times, Gudgeon and his counsel had an equally good answer."

"Being what?" asked Green.

"As I recall it, Counsel asked if initiative tests were ever carried out in his battalion training. The Colonel said that they were and that every CO set great store by encouraging personal initiative in soldiers under their command. Was Major Gudgeon a soldier? Answer, yes. Was he under the Colonel's command? Answer, yes. So what had the Colonel to say about Major Gudgeon—an officer bearing quite a load of responsibility—using his personal initiative? Was it encouraged or not? Of course, the Colonel could see which way the wind was blowing, but he had to agree that a company commander was expected to use a high degree of personal initiative. Such as that shown in getting out with his troops in the danger spots to see what the problems were."

"So Gudgeon got off on all counts, did he?"

"Absolutely, and there were some people, notably the General who had sat as President of the court martial and his Judge Advocate General's adviser, who said very strongly that the charges should never have been made.

But their finding and opinion didn't really help Gudgeon later."

"Why not?" asked Berger.

"Well, I can only tell you what the Chief surmised, because none of it was on paper and we didn't even have a verbal report about it."

"I'll take what his nibs surmised as fact, for the moment," grunted Green. "Carry on, lad, after you've handed over one of your fags."

Reed did as he had been asked and went on: "The Chief thought Gudgeon had been pushed out."

"Out of the army?" asked Berger incredulously. "After he'd been found not guilty?"

"There's more than one way of skinning a pig," grunted Green.

"That's what the Chief thought. He reckoned Gudgeon was told—very informally, of course—that even though he'd been cleared, when it came to promotion, well, he'd have had it. There are always so many candidates that a board looks for any excuse to eliminate a name, and the mere fact that an officer had been deemed worthy of hauling before a court martial would weigh against him, irrespective of the result. You see, the boards aren't entirely composed of serving officers when it comes to higher commands, and so political factors count."

"Are you sure the Chief came to that conclusion?" asked Berger.

"Straight up," replied Reed earnestly.

"It doesn't surprise me," growled Green. "And it shouldn't surprise you either, because he got out, didn't he? Or am I wrong about that?"

"He got out," agreed Reed. "The Chief didn't know anything about pension rights and so forth, but he reckoned there were those who saw to it that Gudgeon wasn't given any cause to dig his toes in on that score."

"You mean they bent the rules?"

"There's ways and means," said Green. "If it was made clear that official thinking was that, as a result of his shooting the gunman, he would become the focus of some revenge killing that might endanger other troops, they would be in a position to offer him decent terms to get him out of the firing line."

"Making it seem he resigned at their request for his own safety, you mean?"

"Something of the sort."

"I still don't understand," protested Berger. "I'd got this Gudgeon chap down as a tough, no-nonsense sort of character who wouldn't knuckle down in any circumstances if he was in the right. There must have been some other reason for his resigning."

"There was," said Masters from the door. "Gudgeon had a wife."

The three of them turned at the sound of his voice.

"Hello, George," said Green. "We'd begun to wonder about you. Just about to send out a light-armoured search party to look for you."

"Thanks." Masters threw his coat and flat cap on to a chair. "Ah, I see you have laid on a little refreshment. Good. Any chance of a sandwich, do you think?"

"And you talk about me!" complained Green.

"I had a one-course dinner, and battling against that wind out there would give anybody an appetite."

Reed got up and rang the service bell, while Berger poured Masters a bottle of beer.

"How did you get on, George?"

"I'll give you a full report, Bill. But you were discussing Gudgeon."

"You'd left us in the dark about him."

"Sorry. But he didn't come up until I'd finished eating dinner."

"So you hared off without a word."

"Yes. The fact is, I couldn't believe my eyes when I saw the list. I'd asked for those names because I reckoned that one of those houses near the harbour might be a local base for the operations we're interested in, and I thought we'd have to ask questions of everybody along

24

there. And what did I see? The name of a man who has served time."

"Bingo?"

"I didn't think so, but I had to make sure."

"And have you made sure?"

"I don't know. I'll discuss it with you."

"Thanks. I'd begun to wonder when we were going to be told something." Green held up his hand before Masters could reply. "I know I always pretend to bellyache about not being told things. This time though, I've held off because I know you've been told to play it close to your chest. But now I reckon I can say, and mean it, that I can see no point in us being here with you if we're not told something about the case we're supposed to be investigating."

"You're absolutely right, Bill, and I had intended to hold a briefing session up in my room after dinner. But this Gudgeon business came up and it seemed to me to be important."

"I've no doubt it was. That means I've got another complaint. You went off alone. It could have been dangerous. As I knew nothing of what you were about, I couldn't even warn you to be careful, let alone do anything to ensure your safety."

Masters nodded. "I suppose I deserve your censure, Bill, but I honestly didn't believe I could be walking into danger."

"No? Going to visit a convicted killer who, if the fact that he lives where he does means anything, could well be entertaining a few more villains? And it wouldn't be very difficult on a night like this for them to have lost you over the sea wall. You can't have it all ways, George. If it was important enough for you to rush off to see Gudgeon, it was important enough to take proper precautions."

"I suppose I took a bit of a risk, but knowing Gudgeon as I think I do, danger wasn't very much in my mind."

"He's killed, hasn't he? Twice?"

"Yes. And that sounds worse that it was, in fact."

"We've heard about the first time, when he shot a gunman in Northern Ireland. Sergeant Reed was telling us he got out of the army, one way or another."

Masters put his drink down. "There is no doubt in my mind that he was pushed. Being the man he is, he would never have agreed to go if it hadn't been for his wife. He was thirty-four at the time, and he'd married a girl in her middle twenties. To say he was besotted with her would be putting it mildly. And I must admit I could see why. She was a stunner, but she was absolutely the wrong wife for a soldier, in my opinion."

"In what way?"

"She was a sensitive creature, like an overbred race-horse. Nervous temperament. Loved Gudgeon, but loathed, not his profession exactly, but the danger and killing and such in Ireland."

"I get it, and the reason for your remark when you came in. Gudgeon took what was coming for his wife's sake."

"It seemed a good idea. He'd got a bob or two stashed away. His people had left him their house and belongings. They'd been sold for a fair sum and Mrs Gudgeon had a little money, too. From an insurance policy, I seem to remember. Anyway, with what they'd already got, and his money from the army and the job he managed to land, they could live quite nicely. They got a house—nice little place standing alone—in Putney, and they were having a fine time making it fit for a king. Because I can tell you, anything Gudgeon set his hand to, he does well, and his wife just loved playing at houses."

"Loved? Past tense?"

"Yes. He came home late one evening to find two unwelcome visitors. His training, I think, made him realize there was something wrong before he got inside. So he went in pretty stealthily, to find his wife cowering in a corner and the two villains packing up the best stuff, having broken up a deal more. He got one of them—a

26

karate chop on the side of the neck. The other managed to escape."

"The first one was dead?"

"That's right. It was in the Met area, so Reed and I were called in."

"And you arrested him."

"I had no choice. The one who escaped said they hadn't attacked Mrs Gudgeon, and she said they hadn't actually touched her. Gudgeon himself, simple soul, didn't realize that an Englishman's home is not his castle and that villains who break in have to be treated with kid gloves. He trusted to the court to find him not guilty of anything, and the court taught him different. He was sent down for manslaughter."

"Just like that?"

"No," said Reed. "It wasn't just like that. The Chief tried to save him from himself, but Gudgeon wouldn't play."

"In what way?"

"Mainly that he wouldn't express any remorse and told the judge that, no matter what the outcome, he'd do the same again and so would any other Englishman worth his salt. And as he'd been asked to swear to tell the truth he saw no point in telling a load of lies about his feelings."

"Not the sort of attitude calculated to endear him to the judge," said Green.

"Actually, defence counsel let him in for it," said Masters, "but it was prosecuting counsel who pulled one of the dirtiest tricks I've ever seen in a British court."

"Why? What went on?" demanded Green.

"Defence counsel had made sure Gudgeon had no police record that could be brought in against him. After the prosecution had finished with me, he got up and asked me straight out if I knew whether the dead man had had a record. I, of course, said that he had been through our hands three times, on each occasion on a charge involving violence against the person. That was to make the point that Gudgeon had not been dealing

27

with a couple of school kids. Then, to point the contrast, he asked me if Gudgeon had a clean character and I answered that he had. Now those questions were permissible, because the first was on a point of fact about a dead man, and the second was brought out by Gudgeon's own counsel, where the prosecution would not have been allowed to ask about the defendant's past record.

"But as soon as the defence had opened that door, prosecution could use it, too. It was Frameby who was prosecuting. . . ."

"That bastion of society!" growled Green. "He ought never to have been allowed."

"Allowed what?" asked Berger.

"Allowed, lad, allowed!"

"To live," said Reed quietly. "He's the joker who will never normally accept a prosecution case."

"Which is his prerogative, of course," said Masters. "There are several eminent men who take that line and stick to it. The fact that Frameby broke his own rule and agreed to prosecute in Gudgeon's case could be viewed, in my opinion, as an indication of some form of personal bias on his part."

"Which you suggest he showed in court?" asked Green. "Not that I'd disbelieve you, having come up against Frameby myself more than once, but I'd like to know how this bias manifested itself."

"One had to be present to appreciate it fully," said Masters, "because one can't do it justice in reporting it. However, I'll try.

"As I said, Frameby was free to question Gudgeon about his past as defence counsel had done so earlier." Masters thought for a moment and then enacted a small scene, playing both parts himself.

"Frameby. 'Some two years ago, Major Gudgeon, I believe you killed a man in Northern Ireland?'"

"Gudgeon. 'Yes.'"

"Frameby. 'You admit you shot a man? Or should I say a youth of sixteen?'"

"Gudgeon. 'That's right. But. . .'"

"Frameby, interrupting. 'When the body of the youth was picked up some moments later, there was no sign of a weapon on or near him. Is that correct, Major Gudgeon? Please answer yes or no.'"

"Gudgeon. 'We found no weapon.'"

"Frameby. 'Thank you. The affair was the subject of a police enquiry, I believe?'"

"Gudgeon. 'It was. An enquiry at which. . .'"

"Frameby. Interrupting. 'Thank you, Major Gudgeon. There is no need to amplify your replies. You have admitted to firing, deliberately, at a youth of sixteen and killing him, and you have, equally frankly, admitted killing a man in your own home. Do you regret those killings?'"

"Gudgeon. 'Not in the least. In similar circumstances I would do the same again.'"

Masters took out his pipe and tin of Warlock Flake. "That is not an exact word for word copy of the transcript, but I can promise you that Frameby's interruptions were just as I've told it. Never once did he allow Gudgeon to inform the court that the police enquiry had completely exonerated him from all blame in the Irish shooting, but rather he used his considerable verbal powers to suggest that Gudgeon was a remorseless taker of human life whenever the opportunity arose."

"But surely," expostulated Green, "defence counsel could reexamine and put the record straight."

"Of course he could, and did. Or rather, he tried. The damage had been done, you see, and Gudgeon hadn't helped by declaring he'd do the same again in like circumstances. He refused to declare a remorse he didn't feel."

"An honest man, in fact."

"An angry one. In Ireland he'd fired to protect his soldiers, after one of them had been hit. In his home he struck a man who had terrified his wife for whom, as I told you earlier, he felt a great and protective love. He wouldn't accept even the possibility of his having done any wrong."

"Understandable," grunted Green.

"Quite. There was also one other factor that I don't believe anybody in that court ever considered. Gudgeon was a highly trained soldier. Hair-trigger trained to react in the face of danger not only to himself but to those for whom he was responsible. I'm not suggesting that courts should ever use that as an excuse, but such men are our servants and we require them to be highly trained and to react positively and quickly. That fact should be taken into consideration when comparing a man like Gudgeon with a common villain who uses violence for gain."

"Agreed," grunted Green. "So he was sent down, was he?"

"For five."

"Five? Who was the judge?"

"Waggers. But he burnt his fingers. On appeal it was cut to three and the appeal court was pretty scathing about Waggers' sentencing. The day after Gudgeon's case, he gave a man who beat and maltreated a three-year-old child over a period of six months—to the point where the child died from his injuries—a four-year sentence. The appeal court said they had difficulty, after hearing both appeals, in reconciling the two sentences. So Gudgeon got three and then earned full remission."

"So he's not out on licence or parole?"

"No. He's in the clear. And has been for over two years."

"And his wife?"

"Dead. After he was sentenced she committed suicide."

"Why? Couldn't face the years without him?"

"That, but I think she blamed herself for his situation. Foolishly, of course. But she said to friends that if it hadn't been for her he'd have stayed in the army, and the incident wouldn't have happened. And also she came to realize that if she'd said the villains had physically manhandled her—because they'd done worse than that, they'd caused her grievous mental harm—her husband could well have got off."

"So what did she do? Take an overdose?"

Masters nodded.

"And now we've got one highly embittered ex-con living alone just down the road?"

"He is certainly bitter, but after making allowances for his experiences, I was pleasantly surprised by his attitude."

"Don't tell me he welcomed you with open arms."

"No, he didn't. But eventually he listened to me. I believe he has an ingrained appreciation of the fact that people like us have to do our duty, however unpleasant, just as he had to in the past. So he didn't blame me too much. In fact, he gave me a couple of shots of whisky."

"Did he! And here's us been worrying about you and laying on a tray of beer."

"Thanks."

"Now, what about this conference in your suite?"

"Tonight?"

"Why not? Nobody's got to get up early as far as I can see. We don't even know what we're here for, let alone if there's anything for us to do."

Masters got to his feet. "If Reed and Berger would replenish the tray. . . ."

"There's a night porter, Chief."

"Good. Bring the stuff up to my suite. We'll see you there."

2

Masters, unusually for him, had booked a suite at the Water's Edge Hotel for just this purpose. He had envisaged conferences. Probably endless ones, and he had been told to do what he had to do at all costs. So he had taken his orders literally. A suite was much more expensive than a single room with bath, even at this out-of-season time. But the additional room had four armchairs as well as a table with four upright chairs, and would serve his purpose very well.

"I'm not intending to overburden you with too much information tonight. The bare bones will be enough to sleep on."

"Uncomfortable mattress, Chief, bare bones," said Berger.

"More comfortable than the bed of nails you'll have when you know everything." He began to rub a flake of Warlock in his hands. "You may remember that in January '83, as a result of the Chief Inspector of Constabulary's report concerning the handling of the Ripper case, the then Home Secretary ordered that provision should be made for setting up teams of the best available investigating officers, with forensic and computer support, to bust major crime —linked crimes was the term used, actually—that crossed over various police force borders."

"I remember," said Green. "A senior investigating officer to be in overall charge. That sounds as if we could be one of those teams, and that you're the boss."

"I was appointed some time ago, actually," said Masters. "And before you ask why you haven't been informed before this, I had better explain that I was ordered to keep the matter secret and the category for the whole operation is, and will remain, Ultra Secret. I have worked alone for some time, as I said, because of this category and because until I'd got a whiff of something to get my teeth into, all I could do was think about the problem.

"As soon as I felt I was ready to do some field work, I informed Anderson that I was ready to choose my team. He could do nothing but agree because he has been ordered to co-operate blind."

"Meaning?" demanded Green.

"That even he is not to be told what we're about unless and until I consider it necessary to tell him and I am given permission to do so."

Green grimaced. "But we are to know?"

"From now on, everything. Naturally I chose you three as my immediate team. You all know our forensic man. He helped us over the botulism affair."

"Doctor Moller? Harry Moller?" asked Reed.

"He's been warned and is standing by to help should we need him. The only other person I have asked for, and have got, is DCS Pollock."

"From Truro?"

"Yes. I wanted a man from these parts, and we've all worked with him. He, too, has been warned to drop everything and come running should I call."

"High-powered stuff," grunted Green. "I shan't mind seeing old Fred Pollock again. He came good in that missing witness case. He'll play along, George. He did last time."

"He was a pleasant man to work with," agreed Masters. "And that, so far, is the whole of the team. It goes without saying that, unless I had every confidence in the three of you, I would have been obliged to choose other officers." He turned to Green. "I had a bit of trouble getting agreement for you to come along, Bill, because technically you are no longer a member of CID. I hope that you'll agree to work as one of the team. We should value your help and. . . ."

"Just try and cut me out," murmured Green, embarrassed by this semi-public recognition of his worth. "We're all happy you stuck with the old firm, aren't we, lads?"

"Good. That's settled then. The name of this operation is 'Hosepipe,' by the way. 'Operation Hosepipe.' Everything to do with it will be referred to by the code-name. And there's one fault we four must correct. We have often, as we did this evening, discussed things relating to our work, or even our work itself, in a public hotel room or bar. We have always been discreet about it, and kept it among ourselves, but with Hosepipe there must not be one word uttered in public places. We can talk in here, in the car, or even when outside, so long as we are isolated. Berger, you will be official scribe. You will write up the general reports and keep the files, which will at all times be kept in the portable safe-box I asked Reed to bring along. All documents in there, please, at all times. You will take it with us in the car when we go out, and you will lock it in your room when we are indoors. There is a combination lock as well as two locks that open with keys. Each of you sergeants will have a key, and we will all know the combination. Be very particular about the index, Berger, and you have my full authority to demand individual reports from whoever works with us at the first possible moment."

"Cross-checking, Chief?"

"A rudimentary system to begin with, in a thumb-paged SO ledger. That will allow you a simple alphabetical index. I don't want bulky card-files or anything of that sort to start with. When we get back to the Yard you may have to set up an incident room proper. But until then nothing; though, if the need does become vital while we're out and about, we'll get an office truck. One of those new, anonymous ones that have their own mobile phones and the facility to tee-in to GPO lines at the drop of a hat."

Green slumped back in his chair. "Now all that side of the business is sewn up, what's the score?"

"Probably the biggest crock of gold still to be obtained in the world is at stake," replied Masters. "That's one way of putting it. There are others. The biggest anti-social crime of all time is intended, a serious financial loss to our own country is being planned, a blow to millions of people is being cooked up . . . how many more descriptions do you want? There is skullduggery mixed up in it, probably murder, certainly kidnapping, industrial espionage and political villainy. I could go on."

"Don't bother," said Green. "Those few will do for starters, just so long as you explain a few of them."

"Quite simply, Rutland Laboratories, a totally British-owned and highly innovative pharmaceutical company, is a long way down the road to perfecting a cure for cancer."

"And?"

"There are those who are out to pre-empt them by pinching the work."

"I can see how important a discovery like that is," replied Green. "Anybody could. But the world presumably wouldn't suffer. The stuff would still be marketed or copied or whatever and made available. All it seems to me is that the gold from the crock you mentioned would go into the wrong pockets."

"Perhaps I'd better explain more fully," said Masters. "The search for the cure is a huge and costly exercise in biotechnology, a job for molecular biologists who are, as you may gather, specialists in the nuclear field. Every country in the world is tackling the problem, and no one has come up with the answer except Rutland Laboratories. They have spent over fifty million on it so far, and have been working on the project for over ten years.

"Quite naturally, they want to get that money back, and more, as a return on the investment. They estimate they are still two years from being able to make the final product available. When they do, the world wide demand for it will be huge and even more important, continuing.

It will also be immediate, because the patients who need it can't afford to wait. Rutland estimates that the demand, before any competitor can build a plant and hope to compete, will be so great that even by selling such a product at a price low enough for all cancer sufferers, worldwide, to afford, they will be more than recompensed for their outlay and skill."

"I should think so," said Berger. "I mean, what would be a low price to be cured of cancer?"

"Quite. Compared with the vast sums spent by every government and individual patient on the measures that can now be taken, almost any price would be cheap. But that is by the way. The company would obviously benefit, but so would this country, hugely, and there would be thousands of jobs in the factories—in packaging, dispatching and so on—expensive hospitals freed for other purposes, skilled doctors made available to tackle other diseases. The list is endless and the advantages incalculable. And somebody is out to dish it. Not as the DCI has suggested, in order to benefit the world, but in order to blackmail it."

"Could you explain that bit, Chief?" asked Reed.

"Pour us all out some more beer, lad, so that his nibs can wet his whistle. And while you're at it, you can give me one of your fags."

"You've got plenty of your own."

"I shall want those for tomorrow morning if this is going to be a long session."

"That remark had the great value of being absolutely meaningless."

"Had it?" asked Green artlessly, taking the proffered cigarette. "In what way, lad?"

"Why will you want all the fags you've got in your packet for tomorrow morning?"

"Did I say that?"

"Particularly if this is going to be a long session? If you want all those for tomorrow morning, it won't make any difference whether tonight's session will be long or short."

"It will, lad, it will."

"In what way?"

"To your packet, of course. I shall smoke a lot more of yours if we sit here jawing for hours than I would if we were to go to bed quite soon—say, after we've finished the beer."

"I should have known better," groaned Reed.

"Funny how some lessons take a long time to learn, isn't it, lad?" Green raised his glass. "Cheers. Here's to me and my wife's husband."

Reed returned to Masters. "You were talking about somebody trying to blackmail the world, Chief."

"I'll try to simplify it for you. As I've said, Rutland have already worked for over ten years on this project. That may seem a long time to you, but I am assured that in the field of medicines, ten years or even the twelve they think it will take to complete, is not much above the average for any major drug. Even minor drugs, I'm told, take a minimum of seven years to discover and get right.

"Now drugs are products which are patented, just like other inventions. For obvious commercial reasons, some of which we have touched on, they have to be so. But there are anomalies in our patents acts when it comes to foods and drugs. More about that later.

"You would think any drug manufacturer with a big new drug on his hands would slap a patent on it at the first possible moment, to ward off competitors. That does not happen for several reasons. Once you take out a patent, your processes, materials and methods are there on paper for all to see. Anybody can go to the patents office and read the whole thing. And competitors—some, at least—do just that, because they know that the slightest deviation from your method or in your materials will get them past the patent laws. I mean, if you use malt vinegar in your process and somebody reckons he can make as good a product using lemon juice, he's free to do so, using all your know-how, without breaking the laws."

"You mean they hold off patenting their discoveries, Chief?"

"Just that. They rely on secrecy to protect their products right up to the very last moment. Then, at least, they know they are away to a flying start. But that is only one of the hurdles faced by drug manufacturers. As I said, there are anomalies in the law concerning foods and drugs. They are these. Once you have taken out a patent for a new type of jam or a new analgesic, say, any other manufacturer in your field can demand as of right to make your product under licence. And he'll get that licence just so long as his manufacturing facilities are up to standard. Such a licence means that the new manufacturer pays the innovator a nominal sum on each article for the use of the patent—say a penny on each bottle of a hundred tablets or some such sum."

"That's grossly unfair, Chief."

"Sometimes, yes. But by and large it prevents monopolies in drugs and foods, both of which are considered vital to life. So there can be no artificial shortages and black-marketeering, such as there were in continental countries crying out for penicillin after the war."

"It sounds basically fair," grunted Green.

"The one other anomaly is that, in addition, with foods and drugs, patent protection only lasts for twenty years. After that, anybody can join in free. But patent age starts from the day the patent is taken out. If Rutland had rushed to patent their cancer cure at the outset, ten years of that patent age would have passed by now, with another two to go before it is in the hands of doctors. That would leave a mere eight years. . . ."

"Against forever if one patented a new rolling-pin?" asked Green.

"Quite."

There was a moment or two of silence and then Masters continued.

"Most industrialized countries are bound by treaty to respect the patents and copyrights of others who are party to the agreements. But there are many countries in Africa, South America and the Far East who do not recognize our patent laws."

"Ah," said Green. "I see what you've been thinking, George."

"Yes, Bill, and my thoughts—about countries not party to patents agreements, I mean—form my working theory."

"Now we're getting to the nitty-gritty, are we?"

"Speculation, I said, Bill. I've been churning this around in my old mind for weeks on end now. It seems reasonable that I should have come up with some theory—be it right or wrong."

"Understood."

"Theory, then. Some nationalistic state, in one of the areas I have specified, has somehow rumbled Rutland's secret. They reckon that the prestige of having the cancer cure, and the money to be made from it,would be immense.

"So they set out to get hold of the specifications, they then patent them in their own country. They then announce they have the cure, and that the patent is held in their capital, but they don't allow patent inspections. In other words, they're going to keep the secret."

"No good," said Green firmly. "Rutland would still have that information."

"Ah," said Masters, "though you are right, Bill, there are complications."

"How come?"

"Rutland have the cure now. All ready. But in this country, the States, Germany, Japan and indeed all the westernized countries, there are committees on the safety of drugs who will not allow any medicine to be used before it has been thoroughly tested. That is why Rutland's next two years are needed. After that—and I'm not exaggerating—more than a hundredweight of paperwork has to be submitted in the form of an application before permission for use can be granted. The submission covers every facet of the drug and all areas of production and testing so that the various government experts can each do detailed checks on every figure, word, process, effect and so on. It's a lengthy and tiresome business for our protection. But our unknown country will have no such inhibitions. They will announce they have a drug which will cure cancer. Can you imagine what will happen? Every one of the hundreds of millions of cancer patients in the world will demand the cure and to hell with government rules, regulations and tests. They haven't got time to wait for two or three years, and as their disease is going to kill them anyway, where's the bonus in holding back to see that it does no harm? So, gentlemen, the cure is announced from the Andes or the Congo or wherever and there is an immediate world furore. And when I say immediate, my guess is that it will happen within hours. After that, can you imagine the Rutland chairman getting up and saying: 'We have a cure, too. I shall patent it today, but you'll have to wait for two or three years before. . .' His announcement would be drowned in the boos, and before he could get to the patent office, some slick London representative of the country in question would be lodging their copy of the patent. When Rutland's patent arrived it would be turned away because the identical thing had already been lodged in another name."

"In every patent office in the world, in fact. Simultaneously," said Green.

"Just so, Bill. And it will be no use Britain complaining. All the westernized countries will know who discovered the drug. But there'd be an outcry from all except a few of the third-world countries. Big, bullying Britain claiming the kudos that some banana republic has well and truly earned for itself. And our political enemies will join in, Bill, just for the sake of scoring points.

"The new owners will be swamped with demands, even from here and America, because how can any government refuse to allow its dying citizens the chance of life? And there'll be no licences granted either. They'll stick to their patent and they'll make every attempt to ensure that people like Rutland can never produce the drug—by legal means or by . . . well, how big a job is it to blow up a production plant?"

Berger said: "You've painted quite a picture, Chief. Of course, I suppose none of us can deny it is a possibility. And when something like this is even a possibility it means that it's credible, and that we've got to look into it."

"Thank you," said Masters. "I got the gist of that, and I'm glad of the support you've offered. Can I say, in this connection, that I have been unable to find another tenable theory? I know that is a negative point, but each one of us could think up alternatives which seem possible for just so long and which then fall down for some reason or another. Or so I believe. Now, to me, a negative point such as this, seems to strengthen the likelihood of my being right. However, few of us are our own best critics, so I'd like all three of you, please, to consider, after you get to bed or when you're shaving in the morning, firstly, what holes you can shoot in my theory and, secondly, possible alternative theories. I've already said I can't find one, so think hard, please."

"Is that it for tonight, George?"

"It's after one o'clock, Bill. I think we've had enough for today. There's a hell of a lot of talking still to do and a few things to look into as well. If the wind stays strong, it may be better to remain indoors and confer tomorrow and then get out and about when the weather is calmer." He got to his feet. "Goodnight, gentlemen. I suggest we don't meet for breakfast until eight o'clock."

Green was down to breakfast first and had already been served with his Victorian platter when Masters joined him.

"You're late, George. For you, that is. Were you lying awake thinking for hours after we left you?"

"No, Bill. I slept from the moment I got into bed. But I've put in a couple of long distance calls already."

Masters turned to the waiter who approached him and

asked for orange juice and scrambled eggs. He then turned back to Green who had wisely—and uncharacteristically—not spoken while the waiter was near.

"Phone calls, George?"

"No developments, Bill. I told you Fred Pollock was to co-operate with us and that we can call on the services of Harry Moller from Dean Ryle Street. They have both been warned—and their respective bosses—that they may be called upon at a moment's notice. I've decided to call them in."

"Eck dum?"

"Pollock is to drive over from Truro this morning."

"Alone, I take it?"

"Strictly alone. Not even his CC knows where he's going."

"How much does he know?"

"Who? Pollock or his CC?"

"Pollock."

"Very little. I wrote him a confidential note after he got the Home Office warning. I said little more than the fact that I had been appointed to head an enquiry—for purposes which I didn't specify—and that I had asked personally for his help. After he got it, he phoned me at the Yard. He very wisely said nothing about the job. He merely said he had got my letter, that it had pleased him to receive it and that he hoped to see me soon. I got him at home this morning. All I said to him was that you and I were staying here for a bit of a holiday and suggested he join us for a night or two. Again he was commendably uninquisitive. He said he would be delighted to join us and we could expect him in time to take a pre-lunch noggin off us."

"And Moller?"

"He knows slightly more about things. On the technical side only. I told Rutland that I had to know something of their processes and that my scientific adviser had to be briefed with as much information as they could let him have whilst still retaining secrecy. I also told them . . ."

Masters broke off as the waiter backed his way through the double door from the kitchen and then turned to head towards the table.

"Those lads are a bit late," said Green, cutting a slice from a sausage. He put the piece in his mouth and forked up a dollop of fried potato, faintly coloured with egg yolk. "Good grub, this," he said to the waiter, furthering his effort to show that the table conversation had been mere chit-chat and had not been broken off at the man's appearance.

When they were alone again, Masters said: "I'm guilty of breaking my own rules. We should stop talking shop immediately."

Green grunted through his mouthful of food. Masters took this to mean that Green would prefer him to finish off what he had been saying. So he continued: "I told Rutland that although they could maintain their secrecy, I would not be fobbed off with anything less than a useful working knowledge. There's not a word on paper, you see, Bill. There are bench notes, of course. They are kept in a safe at all times when not actually in use, so there was nothing they could give us to read and they asked that we should not take notes when they talked to us. I'd guessed that was what they would do, that is why I wanted Moller present. Being a forensic man, he'd be able to understand and remember more than I could. Actually he's a very good investigative scientist. A regular boffin."

"And he's coming here today?"

"Arriving at Taunton at about one o'clock. Reed can meet him. We'll get him to brief everybody this afternoon."

"Fair enough. Ah! We've got company at last." Green looked up at the two sergeants. "Got your beauty sleep in, did you?"

"Yes, thanks," said Berger. "Eventually."

"Meaning?"

"It's these twin rooms," complained Reed. "The Chief sets you a problem before you go off to bed so you lie awake for a couple of hours arguing, trying to solve it before finally throwing in your hand. Past three it was, before . . ."

"I dropped off in mid-sentence," confessed Berger. "After having got precisely nowhere."

"Take your time over breakfast," said Masters. "The DCI and I will be in the lounge."

Masters got to his feet and, accompanied by Green, went through to the lounge and chose a family of four chairs close to a window that looked out to sea.

"Still nasty," remarked Green.

"A little better though."

"If you say so, but look at that dirty great roller creaming in."

A voice behind them said: "You might find the wind will drop a bit as the tide goes out, gentlemen." It was the young hotel manager doing his morning round and making a point of having a word with what few guests he had. "It never lasts long. Not as bad as last night, that is."

"How does it affect shipping in the estuary?" asked Masters.

"They try to stay in dock. Most of it is in and out of Bristol, you see, and it's more comfortable there."

"I'll bet," said Green. "The QE2 would roll in that lot."

The manager passed on to speak to the only other two people in the lounge. They were both immersed in newspapers, so his greetings were brief. Masters and Green followed suit. They were reading papers when Reed and Berger joined them.

Masters put his paper down.

"We will drive along the esplanade towards the harbour," he said. "We can then find a place to park and talk in the car or alternatively use one of those shelters." He indicated the brown-painted Edwardian buildings spaced out along the deserted sea front. "They have four sets of seats, each facing a different way and all divided from each other, so one side should be sheltered from

44

the wind. Anyhow we can try one. It'll be less stuffy than the car."

"Good idea," said Green. "I've got my thermal underwear on and they say sea air is so bracing."

"Five minutes then to get coats and hats," said Masters. "Or has anybody got a more pressing need?"

"We know you're talking about going to the nearest shop for fags," said Green. "But. . . ."

In less than ten minutes Reed was saying: "I can park anywhere along here, Chief. On the seaward side, that is. There are pay and display meters. . . ."

"Ignore them, lad. There's not a sign of any other blessed motor along the whole of this front," said Green. "And if any local bobby comes along in his Panda car, I'll put a pound to a penny he won't get out of it in this weather just to see if you've got a little sticker on your quarter light. If he does, you can always pull rank on him."

"Pull in opposite a shelter, please," said Masters.

Reed complied, and they crossed the dozen yards of grass, leaning into the wind, to get under the lee of the shelter.

"Not bad," grunted Green. "These slatted seats will give us posterior striping, of course."

"Not if you've got your thick woollies on," said Berger.

"Take the corner," said Masters, "then we can sit two and two at right angles and be more of a group. It will make conversation easier." Then, before he sat down, he felt in his pocket for change and selected two ten pence pieces. "I agree with what the DCI said about paying for parking, Reed. But on second thoughts I think we'll pay and display. I don't want any local bobby to get too inquisitive and to know who we are." He handed over the money. "This secrecy business is a full-time chore."

Reed made his way to the nearest meter. While they waited for him, Masters rubbed a palmful of Warlock Flake and filled his pipe.

"First things first," he said when all four were seated.

"Reed, you will go to Taunton to pick up Dr Moller. You know him by sight. He will arrive on the twelve fifty from London. Moller will have a sandwich on the train, so you get something to eat while you're waiting for him, because it could be too late for lunch by the time you get back here and, in any case, I want a full conference this afternoon."

"Right Chief. If I could get away at half past eleven. . . ."

"When you like, but before that you can take Berger back to the hotel. DCS Pollock will be arriving sometime before lunch. I want Berger to meet him and keep him happy until the DCI and I get back."

Berger nodded.

"Now then, to business. There's nobody to overhear us and even if there were, this wind would blow our words away."

"You're going to bring us up to date, George?"

"More or less. Please appreciate that there are very few facts to work on, and so much of what I'm about to tell you is the result of my own thinking."

"Fair enough, Chief. Because quite honestly, Sergeant Berger and I could get nowhere last night."

"Nor me," said Green. "I didn't have enough gen to work on."

"Sorry about that. What you're now about to hear might help. I'll start off with one fact, at least.

"The Rutland Company, as you can imagine, employs a strong team of high-powered scientists. One of the leading lights in their research team was a molecular biologist, called Arthur Hopcraft. Actually he was Doctor Hopcraft, aged thirty-two."

"Was?" queried Green. "What's happened to him?"

"That is part of our problem, Bill. He disappeared, and it was his disappearance that alerted Rutland to the fact that their secret was no longer entirely their own."

"And that's their only proof that something has leaked out?"

"No. But more will come out as we go along. I'd like

46

to try and keep things in chronological order for the sake of clarity."

"Best way," agreed Green, reaching across him to help himself to a cigarette from the packet Berger had just taken from his pocket.

"Hopcraft was an unmarried man and, as I said, a biologist. When he took leave from the laboratory, he went off on his own with a backpack as often as not, observing flowers, birds and the like. That was his hobby and he believed the countryside and the tramping were the best ways of blowing away the cobwebs after months of intensive work in a laboratory. That is hearsay from his colleagues and it seems reasonable enough.

"One thing I should interpose at this point is that he was a graduate of Bristol University which, I am given to understand, is world-famous for its high standards in molecular biology, and Hopcraft was reputed to have been among its very brightest products. He was employed by Rutland, straight after getting his doctorate, to work on the then infant cancer-cure project."

"Bristol," murmured Green. "Not all that far from here."

"Quite. That was why I mentioned it. But to carry on. Towards the end of last summer, Hopcraft took a fortnight off to go on one of his usual nature trails. He never returned. Rutland got the wind up and reported his disappearance. We—the police, that is—couldn't assist them.

"In their situation, they could not help but regard his disappearance as sinister. Had his body been found, the matter would have been serious enough for them, in that they were losing the man who knew all about, and, indeed, was leading, their research. But at least they would have known he had met with an accident or had been attacked or drowned and that would have been the end of it. But no body has ever been found."

"So they suspect kidnapping for the sake of what he knew?" asked Reed.

"Precisely. No ransom has been demanded or anything

47

of that nature, so if he was kidnapped it must have been for his knowledge. Now, you asked whether Hopcraft's disappearance was Rutland's only proof that something could have been leaked.

"Their reasoning—and I can't fault it—is that if their research had been documented, the disappearance of Hopcraft would not have appeared so sinister. People intent on getting the information would have made an attempt to steal the documents or, rather, photograph them, without drawing attention to their industrial espionage by pinching the leading scientist."

"Wait a minute," objected Green. "How did the thieves know nothing had been put on paper?"

"Ah! That was a problem for me, to begin with. And then it occurred to me that the only people who would know this, in view of such tight security, were those people who actually worked there, or had done so in the past."

Green stared at him for a moment. Then he said slowly: "It's a question we always have to ask ourselves in any enquiry like this. Is it an inside plot? You went nap on it and decided there had to be an internal leak because there was no chance of an outsider getting to know a fact like that?"

"Yes."

"Fair enough. But identifying the culprit. . . ?"

"Not easy. The answer took a long time to ferret out. So it's a longish story."

"We're listening," growled Green, drawing his coat more tightly about him. "And you're going to tell us anyway, so get on with it. It's as cold as an Eskimo's fridge round here."

Masters grinned. "I scouted around a bit, and the answer came piecemeal. Or what I believe to be the answer. Rutland has a big manufacturing plant north of Birmingham. Attached to it are their research and development laboratories. Ordinary research, that is. The cancer research project was not done there."

"No?"

"They bought a big old house miles from nowhere and set in its own grounds."

"Secretly?"

"No. They were quite open about it. They claimed it was their executive training centre."

"Don't tell me," said Green. "Let me guess. They actually gathered people there for training etcetera, but when they got there they found certain sections of the building were out of bounds. Strictly verboten to visiting executives and trainees."

"Exactly right. The cancer research labs were operating very smoothly with none of the visitors even knowing they were there. In fact, only one or two senior directors did know they were there. It was assumed that the boffins—if they were ever noticed going to or from the building—were members of the training staff."

"Go on," grunted Green. "Something about the set-up must have started you thinking."

"It did. I wondered if their complete secrecy didn't give them away."

"How come, Chief?" asked Reed.

"Just so long as a secret set-up like that is one hundred per cent leakproof, it is perfect, but as soon as it develops a hole as big as a pin head, it is finished. The very measures that have been taken to ensure secrecy show that there is something worth having. Or so I thought. Rutland had been operating there for ten years or so with not a word getting out. So what had happened?

"I turned over in my mind what could be the cause. The sale of information by an employee? Careless chatter and so on? I reckoned that if Hopcraft had sold the secrets, he wouldn't have needed to disappear. If the boffins had chattered, it would more than likely be among themselves, because nobody else but a boffin in the same line would understand them.

"But as somebody apparently had understood them, I looked for another boffin." Masters looked at his companions. "I was a bit slow off the mark here. It should have leapt to my mind immediately that as many secrets as not are divulged in pillow talk."

"A woman, of course," said Berger.

"A woman boffin," amended Masters.

Green sat up straight. "A tasty bit of capurtle to cajole the secrets out of . . . who? Hopcraft? . . . with a trained mind capable of understanding them. It's so bloody obvious, George. . . ."

"I realize that."

"I meant now you've spelt it out. Have you found the woman?"

"I think I may have done so," said Masters slowly. "What I did was to ask for all Rutland's lists of employees, visitors to, and staff of, the secret laboratory and so on. And I sat down with them, just to see whether they showed me anything at all."

"It took me a little time, because I was combing carefully. I was actually rather annoyed to find that the personnel people had supplied lists of different dates. That of the Birmingham employees was some months older than that of the research establishment. But eventually I was thankful they had been too idle to update them. You can probably guess why. I found one name, that of a senior technical secretary, on both lists. Her name was Essa Bari.

"On the face of it, that wasn't much to go on, but as it was all I had, I paid a visit to the personnel director at Birmingham. The Chairman of Rutland, as uneasy as anything about the whole affair, sat in on the interview. Then I asked about Bari.

"A very able woman," I was told. "She had applied two and a half years ago for the vacant post of secretary in the Birmingham Research and Development Department. She had got the job because not only was she an able typist but she could speak fluent Italian, with a good smattering of German and French, which accomplishment, I was informed, was a great asset in an area where foreign papers had to be consulted or even translated.

"I could appreciate this, but somehow it didn't ring

quite true. I asked how it was that a girl so proficient in languages should be content to remain a secretary. I thought she probably had a degree in Italian and so was capable of earning the extra money that this would have brought her in the translation department.

"I was told that her father had been Italian, her mother English, and she had spent most of her young life in Italy."

"Bari—that's the name of an Italian town," said Reed. "Like people in this country are called by place names—Hampton, for instance, or Derbyshire."

Masters nodded. "That seemed straightforward enough. Her photograph was there, and it was obvious that she was a very good looking, dark girl.

"Had they asked to see her passport?—the personnel man said there had been no need to do so. He never asked to see passports, only degree certificates and the like from technical executives.

"Why had she moved to the cancer research house?—because a vacancy had arisen there. The senior secretary had resigned for some reason, and because of the isolated position of the house it was not easy to recruit suitable clerical staff. So, whenever this problem arose they tended to offer such jobs to people employed at Birmingham—to single girls with no particular ties, who were willing to go rural for the sake of a few extra pounds a week. Miss Bari had fitted the bill and accepted the job.

"I almost left it there, but I asked where Miss Bari was now, and I was told she had left the company. When I asked why, I was told she had gone back to Italy to marry, soon after Hopcraft had disappeared."

Green shifted on the hard seat. "That sounds reasonable enough on the face of it, George."

"True. But I was looking for chinks in the Rutland armour, Bill. However unpromising, it was the only lead I had. So I asked the Chairman to take me to the research house. In his presence, I interviewed his boffins one by one. It aroused no suspicions. They all thought

51

it was time the police started to do something about Hopcraft, so they co-operated without question."

"And?" asked Green.

Masters turned to him. "You know how it is sometimes, Bill. Pure chance if you're told some little thing that helps. Equally pure chance if you recognize it as such. Those boffins may be a bit abstracted at times, but they notice things. They actually gave me three bits of valuable information."

"The first was that Miss Bari and Hopcraft became pretty matey. Understandable, because he was single and she was good looking. Anyhow, they were known to be sleeping together."

"Pillow talk, you said, Chief," reminded Reed.

"That was my original thought," admitted Masters, "but I am not too sure I was right. I believe that Hopcraft kept his lip buttoned. But those boffins are dedicated men—even brave men, in so far as they are usually prepared to use the drugs they invent on themselves just to make sure they have no ill effects on the human body. Hopcraft was injected in the arm one day—self-injected—and he made a bit of a hash of it. He tore the skin and it bled. He told his colleagues the next morning that Miss Bari had been mighty curious about it in bed that night. He said he reckoned he had fobbed her off. But gentlemen, I was of the opinion that if a company's main research lab is in Birmingham, yet they are maintaining a secret place in the country where there are obviously high-powered boffins who inject themselves with their own products, that fact would scream aloud that there was something going on they were desperately anxious to hide. Something valuable in other words."

"With you," grunted Green.

"The third titbit I latched onto was a remark by a somewhat older scientist. He had been asked to read a paper at some convention for boffins. Not on Rutland's project, of course, but in the same general area. He told me how wonderful he thought Miss Bari was. He was an execrable writer and his manuscript was full of highly

52

technical terms which he thought no typist would be able to understand or decipher. Yet Miss Bari had typed it for him without making a mistake and without having to ask a single question. As I said, the boffin thought that was wonderful. I thought it highly suspicious."

"In what way, Chief?"

"I reckoned it would need another boffin to type the first boffin's paper so perfectly. It suggested to me that Miss Bari was not just a secretary with a knowledge of languages."

Green said: "Let's get it straight. You sussed that this Italian raver was a scientist in her own right, disguising herself as an efficient technical secretary?"

Masters nodded. "But you've got to realize, Bill, that it didn't all drop into place, just like that. I spent hours thinking things out. Days, in fact. I actually went round to various departments in the Yard and asked how many of our secretaries got even an ordinary short letter correct one hundred per cent of the time. I was shown files of carbon copies. There'd been a lot of correcting. When I got on to our more technical people—well, their bosses said that for the most part they were very good indeed, but there were a hell of a lot of bosh shots. The word processor supervisor told me that things were a lot better now, because corrections could be made on the screen, but she said the great value of the new machines was that corrections could be made so easily. So, eventually, I came to the conclusion that Miss Bari was a very clever woman, but that she had made the tiny mistake of producing perfect work. A fact which would never be noticed—except perhaps with admiration—were it not that I was looking for any little thing out of the ordinary simply because I had started an investigation."

"Still, Chief," said Berger, "to make capital out of work that was too perfect. . . ."

"Don't forget I was already suspicious of the girl."

"Maybe, Chief. But did it pay off?"

"It must have done," said Reed, "otherwise we wouldn't be here."

"What happened?" asked Green.

"I had enough presence of mind to visit the Rutland Personnel Department again and ask to see the job specification for the work that Miss Bari would be expected to do when she went to her new post at the research centre. I was told there wasn't one. Evidently their secrecy concerning the new work extends to not even providing a job spec for the secretaries there."

"They couldn't claim a lass would take a new job sight unseen, could they?" asked Green.

"That's what I thought. They told me, when I asked, that the girl had been given a verbal description of the job. They admitted, without prompting, that one of the plus points—their words, not mine—they used to persuade her to take the job was that there would be no long, boring research reports to type up. This little fact alone showed that the woman I suspected was aware that no research information was put on paper."

"Before she even took the job."

"Yes."

"Which was probably the reason why she accepted it."

"Maybe. She wanted to get inside, though, whatever went on to paper—in my opinion."

Green nodded his agreement. "That's answered the question of how the thieves could have got to know there was nothing on paper to steal. And your suspicions about this bit of Italian capurtle were strengthened. What did you do about it?"

"I told you I'd seen a photograph of this girl. These big companies keep Gestapo files on all their employees, you know. So I demanded it and had it copied. Then, quite frankly, I was stumped. I was operating alone and I didn't know where to begin. I couldn't go to her digs because I didn't want to start speculation. That was the bugbear. I could have started all sorts of searches if I'd had the manpower or if I'd been able to tell others what I was about. I might have approached the Immigration Office, Aliens, even the Italian Embassy, but you know the dangers if a chap like myself starts fishing in waters like that."

"It could be that it wouldn't have caused comment."

"I daren't risk it, Bill. But I had to do something, so I approached Robby Lippert."

"Special Branch?"

"Yes. We're old friends, as you know, and I trust him completely, otherwise I would have steered clear. Apparently, he trusts me too," said Masters simply, "or at any rate he asked no questions."

"None at all?" asked Green in disbelief.

"Not one. I showed him the photograph, told him that the name she had been using while working for Rutland was Essa Bari and that she was supposedly of mixed Italian and English parentage; that she had now left Rutland, reputedly to return to Italy to marry; that I wanted to know if this information was correct; that I'd like a run-down on her; that the business was secret and urgent. I added that she spoke good English, Italian, some German, some French, that she was a first-class typist and possibly had some knowledge of the sciences."

"There's one thing," said Green. "If Special Branch was asking the questions, it wouldn't link the case with you, but it could still start speculation, and that would be as bad."

"I think more files are open to them than to us," replied Masters. "At any rate, in less than forty-eight hours Robby met me to say that no such person as Essa Bari had ever been in this country."

"Ah!" breathed Green. "So she came in as somebody else, did she?" He turned to Masters. "And I suppose that little nugget of information told you that you were on the right track?"

"What do you think?"

"I think we should get into the car and continue the conversation in there, while one of the lads drives us to a coffee shop. I've got corns on my backside and I'm frozen stiff."

"Pity."

"Why?"

"Because we are sitting about forty yards from the front door of Major Gudgeon's cottage."

"And? You're not keeping an eye on him, are you?"

"Not specifically. But if we move away, you and I will have to come back again."

"Why?"

"Because I think you'd like to meet him. I thought we might call in when the sergeants go off on their separate jobs. However . . ." Masters got to his feet, "Reed can run us back after you've had your sticky bun."

"Doughnut," corrected Green. "I feel like a doughnut, and. . ." he turned to the sergeants, "anybody who makes a crack to follow that will have to buy my lunch-time drinks."

They crossed to the car. Reed drove along and turned at the cluster of buildings near the end of the quay. Berger, impatient to hear more of Masters' story, asked: "Did SB discover who this Bari woman was, Chief?"

"Within a surprisingly short time—only a matter of a day or two—they came back with the news that they believed her to be Eissa Al Barcurata. She had come to this country as a Libyan-government-sponsored student and had then apparently disappeared."

"Changed her identity, you mean?"

"They could only assume so. Certainly she never attended any classes at university."

"And nobody did anything?"

Masters shook his head. "She was a foreign student who didn't turn up. Her tutor informed the college warden's office. He wrote a letter or two but got no reply. Remember even then Libyan ambassadorial and consular connections in this country were not too hot—and are far worse now—so the college authorities were not surprised and just dropped the matter."

"And Special Branch? Weren't they involved?"

"Apparently not. According to Robby, they can't keep an eye on every foreign student that comes to this country, they assume these people are doing just what they came here to do. They keep an eye on known or suspected thugs, of course, but the college had not informed the police that a foreign student they had expected had not appeared, and so the news had not filtered via ordinary police channels to Special Branch."

"She had flown in, using her own name and a permit to study, some time before the start of term and without clocking in at the college had lost herself?"

"That's it, Bill. And she clocked out again in her own name last September, just as if she'd used up her permit for a three year study course."

"Not to go and get married?"

"No. To fly to Tripoli."

"And she got away with it?"

"She didn't break the law in any of the usual ways to draw attention to herself, Bill. No policeman could get an apparently harmless secretary going about her job for anything, could he?"

"But what about NHS contributions, income tax and so on? Wouldn't their computers show there was something wrong?"

"No, Bill. She was able to masquerade as an Italian after getting here. She didn't present herself as a Libyan. And as long as no prospective employer asked for her passport she would get away with it. Italy is in the EEC and citizens of member countries are allowed to cross borders to work. There is provision made for foreign nationals of member countries to bowl in, sign on without any questions being asked, pay their just dues and demands and then go again. Quite simple. It has to be. Or we reckon it has to be and make it so."

"We're Joe Soap as usual," grumbled Green. "You go and try that lark in Greece for example and see how far you'd get."

Reed turned the car and retraced the route along the sea road. Berger asked: "But she spoke Italian, Chief?"

"That's right. As soon as Special Branch realized what they'd turned up, they began to dig deeper. It took them

57

something like a fortnight to get her life story. She has Italian blood. Her grandfather was one of Mussolini's colonists and her grandmother Tripolitanian. Her father spoke both languages equally well. He married a woman from Tripoli—an educated one—and the resultant daughter, Eissa, was a clever little thing who learned both languages too, and also took a science degree in Egypt. Apparently, after the Italian defeat in forty-three, grandad assumed his wife's family name of Barcurata. The girl is intensely nationalistic, apparently. Our Intelligence people believe her to have been recruited by Gadaffi's mob specifically for industrial spying. As her English was also so good, she was filtered in here under the guise of a student, specifically to get a job in some firm such as Rutland's to do technical typing and keep her very knowledgeable eyes open. It seems she struck oil."

Reed turned right into the main street of Yourhead.

"Baker's shop up on the right," said Berger. "Café sign outside."

"Good enough. Park somewhere near, please."

"Chief," said Berger, as they entered the shop to climb the stairs to the café. "I know we can't talk in here, but I want to hear what comes next."

"Me, too," said Reed. "But if I've got to shove off to Taunton as soon as we've seen the DCI eat his doughnut. . . ."

"Don't worry. I'll continue this afternoon. Our two colleagues need know very little of what I have told you so far, because that is just the preamble. What comes next is how and why we are here. And that's the important thing."

When they got back on to the pavement after coffee, Masters said: "The wind appears to have dropped appreciably."

"Gone out with the tide," said Green knowingly. "It often does that, like the hotel manager said."

"Irrespective of cyclones, anticyclones, which quarter we're in and the closeness of the isobars?" asked Berger, innocently.

"All right, smarty pants. I watch weather forecasts, too. But they give a general picture. They don't pick up the hiccups which occur all the time in general trends, particularly where sea and land meet. Any local fisherman will tell you winds often come in and go out with the tides."

"I'll take your word for it."

"You'd like me to run you along the front again, Chief?" asked Reed.

Masters turned to Green. "Gudgeon's cottage is less than half a mile away. Do you fancy a walk?"

Green looked about him. "Perhaps it would be best," he said at last. "I take it you don't want to draw attention to Gudgeon's place by arriving in a dirty great car with four obvious coppers sitting in it?"

"The thought had struck me."

Green buttoned his coat about him and turned up the collar in preparation for the march. As he and Masters walked towards the sea, Masters gave him a full report of his meeting with Gudgeon the previous evening.

As they turned left to walk along the esplanade, Green said: "It sounds to me as though you showed him something of your hand, George. Was that wise?"

"I felt I had to."

"Why? I mean, he just happens to be here. That business about ex-cons waltzing past his front door and recognizing him is all baloney."

"It isn't, I'm afraid, Bill."

"I see. Something we haven't yet heard about."

"I had intended to get round to it this morning, but the coffee break. . . ."

"So it's my fault, is it?"

"Yes. You asked if we could visit the coffee shop."

Green grunted in acknowledgement of this truth, and then asked: "Are you going to tell me now?"

"Ever heard of a villain called Farries?"

"Sid Farries? So-called strong-arm man, but with the brain of a gnat and the guts of a louse?"

"That sounds like a good description of him. He was siding Dewhurst. . . ."

"Never heard of him."

"He was the character Gudgeon chopped. The brains of the outfit, I'd say. Farries, despite his reputation as a bruiser, scarpered when Gudgeon went into action."

"That fits what I know of Farries. He's a hard man as long as he's on top, but a big bladder of lard when the going gets tough. Has he turned up in this little business?"

"As you would expect, Special Branch got very interested in Eissa Al Barcurata after discovering the few bits and pieces I'd asked Robby Lippert for."

"So he didn't keep it to himself?"

"He did, as far as my investigation was concerned, but Robby explained, and I agreed, that they couldn't have aliens like this woman sculling around the countryside without knowing anything about her and what she was up to. Particularly Libyans who, as we know, have been playing merry hell in parts of the world lately, including London."

"So he dug a bit deeper, did he?"

"I think his superiors directed him to do so, and gave him some assistance from outside the police force."

"Intelligence people?"

"I assume so. I didn't ask, because had I done so I might not have been told. Anyhow, they came up with the information that this girl had been in touch, during the last two months of her time at the research centre, with a thirty-five year old cashier who works in the Bank of Cyrenaica."

"I know it. One of these modern ones that's sprung up in Fenchurch Street."

"That's it. Now Robby and his colleagues keep something of an eye on these new financial institutions because they are staffed for the most part by their own nationals. . . ."

"Who could in turn be something more than ledger keepers. In fact, those banks could be right little hotbeds of alien intelligence."

"As much as embassies are, I suppose. Anyhow, Robby's people—when they saw copies of the photograph I'd given him—turned up the files and identified her as having met the bank cashier twice outside the bank and, probably, several times inside it."

"Pushing under the grill cheques that contained some sort of message? That sort of thing?"

"Maybe. But the interesting thing is that during the time our cashier friend was in touch with Eissa, he was also observed—quite by chance, incidentally—talking on the embankment with Geoff Crease."

"Ah!"

"Obviously a name you recognize."

"Who doesn't? A natty dresser. Ostensibly a legitimate business man, but known to have been the instigator of as much villainy as half the ex-cons in London put together."

"The same. And I am reliably informed by our immediate colleagues at the Yard that Farries has been working for Crease ever since Gudgeon knocked off Dewhurst."

Green grimaced. "That's a very tenuous link, George."

"Admittedly, and you will note that when talking to Gudgeon I emphasized that I thought any villain who might have been operating down this way could have been somebody serving a sentence at the same time as he was. I was very, very careful not to suggest it could have been Farries, and you will guess why."

"I can," grated Green. "From what I've been told about Gudgeon he'd be out looking for Farries if he thought he was here. And before so very long he'd have a third killing to his credit."

"Quite so. Gudgeon is not the sort of man to forgive

Farries for having frighted—and, in her husband's opinion, eventually killed—Mrs Gudgeon. He'd be out after him, as you say, and I don't want that to happen on two counts. One, I don't want him muddying our water and two, I don't want a chap like that going back inside."

"If he did it again he'd be inside for ever."

"I reckon he would. Now, Bill, we'd better forget this conversation for a time. Gudgeon's cottage is only about forty yards along from here."

Green stopped in his tracks. Masters, after going forward a pace or two, turned and asked: "Is something the matter, Bill?"

"Of course there is."

"What?"

"Just the little matter of the reason for us calling on Gudgeon. Or aren't you going to bother to tell me and just let me blunder in."

Masters grinned. "As a matter of fact, I was."

"Thanks."

"I was going to trust to you following your nose, Bill. I value your instinct as highly as I value your opinion and I was hoping the first would give rise to the second, unbidden, as it were. Or rather, without any lead from me. But if you're anxious to know what I'm about. . . ."

"I am."

"I'm not too sure myself, but we'll cross over on to the esplanade, walk towards the harbour and call on Gudgeon as we come back."

"It's not called the esplanade just here," said Green as they crossed the road. "Not this bit of it, between here and the harbour. It's called Quay Street."

They turned to walk along close to the thick, heavily-built sea wall. Neither spoke for a moment or two.

"Not much of a harbour," said Green.

"Only a jetty, really," agreed Masters, "but as it curves so much, it does form a sort of sheltered bay. Not that it matters very much. The hotel manager told me before dinner last night that there's no longer any commercial shipping plying in and out."

"There's a few pleasure-craft on the moorings."

"I think in the summer it gets quite full. Never over-crowded, of course, but there are still all the facilities there, I understand. Steps down to the water, mooring rings let into the stonework. That sort of thing."

"So they can restock and refuel, can they? Before leaving the Bristol Channel for other waters?"

"I imagine so. There are shops and a pub at the entrance to the quay, as you probably saw when we drove down here before going for coffee."

"A gas house, too. There's still an old gasometer."

"I don't think the North Sea variety has got this far, so they still make their own. You'll remember that the pub's very close to the gas house and so is the lifeboat station."

"Ah," said Green. "They actually have a lifeboat, do they? I have a lot of time for the blokes who man them."

Masters didn't add to this sentiment, and after a pause, Green asked: "You still haven't told me why we're calling on Gudgeon, and we shall be turning back in a minute."

"As I told you, Bill, I have no clear idea myself, but I'd like to try something out on him."

"Oh, yes. What?"

"Are you wondering why we are down here in Your-head at this time of the year and with apparently no good reason?"

"Of course I am. But I know so little about any of this lark that I expected it to be one of the things you brought up at the conference this afternoon."

"Quite right. There's a shelter at the beginning of the quay. Let's get in there and I'll give you a brief run-down on why I brought us all here."

They gained the shelter and sat down, protected from what remained of the wind. As Masters filled his pipe, he began to speak. "I am by no means certain that I'm on the right track in coming here, Bill."

"You must have had a good reason for coming."

"What I think are good reasons, yes. But there could

be a large element of wishful thinking in arriving at the decision." He pointed, with the stem of his pipe, straight ahead of him. "That was partly responsible."

"What was?"

"The hill we are looking at."

"I've been wondering about that. It's bloody steep."

"Because it is really a cliff, Bill. It's called Barway Cliff, presumably because it did bar the way in all sorts of directions. What we can see is the end of the cliff formation. In front, facing us, it is practically sheer and, to our left, it slopes a bit more gently down to the flat area where Yourhead has grown up. The cottages opposite are built right under the drop. They have no back entrances to the properties. This part of the esplanade, which you tell me is called Quay Street, runs on past the lifeboat shed and I think—though I haven't been there yet—that there is a certain amount of flat land beyond where we turned the car and then the face of the cliff turns seawards. . . ."

"I can see that," said Green, "but it's so completely covered in trees it's difficult to make out contours and turns. Besides, the buildings are blocking the view from here."

"That's so, but I think the cliff comes to the shore and then continues, away from us, as an actual sea cliff. It turns away out of sight. . . ."

"I get it. Where it touches the shore is actually a corner."

"Right. Now I've said Barway Cliff was partly responsible for bringing us here. The reason for my saying that is because the area—the flat land that lies beyond us a well as the cliff itself—are, I understand, almost a nature reserve."

"Designated?"

"No. It doesn't have to be, because the cliff at any rate is so difficult to negotiate that it has become not only a bird sanctuary, but a haven for all sorts of wildlife. you noted how heavily it is wooded. I've read this up a bit. There are sycamore, Scots pine, sessile oak, evergreen oak, turkey oak, elm, larch, horse chestnut and walnut to name but a few of them up there. Oh, and rowan, elder, ash, hazel, black poplar. . . ."

"Don't go on," grunted Green.

"I don't want to bore you, but there's also every sort of wild flower, undergrowth plants, ferns, birds, butterflies, snails, moths . . . you name it, it's there. In other words, there's everything there to delight the heart of a nature buff, and Hopcraft, don't forget, was a biologist."

"That sort that did his bit of nature study?"

"Very much so. When I was looking into his comings and goings, I found his old nature notebooks for years back. And it seems that Barway Cliff was one of his old stamping grounds."

"Ah! He was a student at Bristol, you said, and that's only a lock of perches higher up the estuary than this place."

"Quite right, Bill. So this became one of his favourite haunts. Now, his colleagues knew, when he took his break late last summer, that he was going on the nature trail again. The trouble is, he didn't say where. And this was not typical of him. Usually he was very open about his movements and chatted to his colleagues about where he was going and so forth. But not this time. He was actually asked his destination and according to his mates, merely answered the question by giving a broad wink."

Green turned and stared at Masters. "A broad wink. That means . . . well, I'd interpret it as meaning he was proposing a bit of hanky-panky. That he wouldn't be doing the trip alone."

"My opinion exactly, Bill."

"There was going to be a girl along, and as he was sleeping with this Libyan piece, it doesn't take much guessing as to who the girl was going to be."

"Right, Bill. Especially as the Rutland leave-list showed Miss Essa Bari as taking ten working days leave at the same time as Hopcraft was absent from his laboratory."

Green trod out the stub of a cigarette. "You reckon he came here?"

"Yes."

"How could you possibly know that?"

"Guesswork, Bill."

"Guesswork? That's rubbish, George, and you know it."

"Not so, Bill. I'm not saying I didn't try to reason it out, but I had no facts to go on. Look, chum, this is the basis for my guesswork. Hopcraft had been abducted or kidnapped or whatever. That was all I knew. But I reasoned that if he had been picked up because of his knowledge of the Rutland research, his captors would want him somewhere other than in this county."

"Why?"

"Because I didn't believe that anybody could set up plant and operate here. Oh, I know they could have forced Hopcraft to tell them all he knew and then could have knocked him on the head. But no body has come to light. I couldn't assume he was dead without some reason for doing so. And besides, in a project of this magnitude, and of a trickiness so great that nobody else in the world could manage it, nobody, not even a nitwit, would kill off the only bloke who knew what it was all about—before the project was on line, that is."

"I'll buy that," grunted Green.

"Then I learned from Robby that Libyans were involved. And not just any old Libyans, but a sponsored one in Miss Bari and an official one in the bank clerk. So, I reckoned Hopcraft could have been carted off to Libya."

"That sounds feasible," agreed Green.

"But still guesswork Bill."

"If you say so. What then?"

"Several bits and pieces started to look as though they could—just could—fit together. I discounted the possibility of the Libyans getting Hopcraft out of the country by air. Tripoli is a hell of a long way away to reach in a light plane such as might be landed at some little unknown airstrip, and I couldn't see them getting our friend through all the checks at Heathrow. I mean, taking a grown man through against his will . . . and I reckoned that a drugged man would be equally difficult to get on board a plane. So I went nap on their getting him away by sea."

"That's not easy, either," asserted Green.

"Maybe not. Now, I didn't know whether Libya had any mercantile marine other than Mediterranean coastal craft. But I checked and found they have two sizeable cargo craft, of about nine thousand tons a piece. They're registered under the Liberian flag, of course, but they are sufficient for Libyan needs—outside exporting oil, which is mostly transported in carriers belonging to the oil firms of importing countries.

"Libya exports very little except oil, of course, but it does import well over two hundred million pounds' worth of goods from the UK."

"What does it send us besides crude oil?"

"This and that. Some wool, horses, esparto grass, olive oil, sponges, hides, skins . . . that sort of thing. In return we send them mainly foodstuffs like sugar, tea and coffee and a fair amount of constructional material and consumer goods."

"Just enough to keep two tramp steamers busy, eh?"

"One would assume so. But more important than what they carry, is where they dock on their visits to the UK."

"Don't tell me," grunted Green. "Bristol."

"Got it in one. So, more guesswork. Gadaffi being the bloke he is, I reckoned that the skippers of those two vessels, and their crews, would all be in his pocket. What I mean is, that if they were ordered by the Libyan government to pick up a bit of supercargo for transfer to Tripoli, there'd be no questions asked."

"Too bloody true," grunted Green.

"You guessed at Bristol as the port of call. That's a few miles further up the Bristol Channel, so any ship leaving there is obliged to steam past Yourhead, two or three miles out in the stream."

Green nodded.

"Of course, I didn't think of Yourhead until I'd seen Hopcraft's notebooks. I'd imagined the villains luring him to Bristol and then secreting him on board in the docks. But after I'd seen the notebooks, it occurred to me that Miss Bari could have seen them, too. I suspected she might have told Hopcraft that she would like to see this area of the country, and seeing he was so keen on it, and was planning a nature holiday anyway, why shouldn't he come here, adding as an inducement that if he agreed to do so, she would come along to share his tent and do the cooking."

"Very, very probably," murmured Green. "An offer he couldn't refuse."

"A boat tied up in the little harbour behind us. A little overnight stowing of human, if inert, cargo. No customs to worry about. A trip out into the estuary—a long way out—and a mid-sea transfer. Easy to make. Wouldn't take more than two minutes to haul him aboard in calm weather. Then the ship ploughs on, and the boat goes as it pleases."

"And that's it, is it?" asked Green.

"Not quite. I was pleased with my theory, but it was still nothing more than guesswork."

"So what did you do to make more sure of your ground?"

Masters laughed. "I stooped to impersonating another police officer."

"Oh, yes? Which one?"

"Old Wally Hardman in Missing Persons. I'd approached him very early on—without giving anything away—and he hadn't been able to help me at all. But now I had a place in mind and I knew the dates covering Hopcraft's disappearance. So I rang the Yourhead station, claiming to be Wally—so as to give nothing away."

"Go on."

"They said they'd no reports of anything untoward during the first fortnight of September. I said I'd not really expected anything, but I had found a chap and his girlfriend who said they'd seen our friend camping somewhere near Barway Cliff. The locals told me that was impossible, as camping isn't allowed there.

"Still . . . I persisted. Anyhow, Bill, the upshot was that they turned to the desk sergeant's book and found that a local bobby had actually reported an empty tent on the flat ground on the morning of the fourth of September. He'd waited a bit, to see if the owner turned up, so as to tell him to move on, but the camper didn't return. The bobby visited the site twice later on the same day, at intervals, but still no camper. So he thought he'd call along very early the next morning before even the keenest camper would be out of bed. But by five the next morning the tent had gone."

"So there was no reason to do anything about it?"

"No reason at all. No action taken, no person missing. Just a usual, everyday, trivial incident."

"But you reckon the tent belonged to Hopcraft."

"Why not, Bill? Abducted the first night. By a couple of thugs like Farries, I suppose. They hadn't enough brain to strike the tent. They left it there. Then somebody with a bit more up top heard about it, thought it might attract unwelcome attention, and had Farries and friend pick it up, by dark, the next night."

"And that's your guesswork, George."

"Never mind that."

"Why call on Gudgeon?"

"He's a man of parts, Bill, and he gets out and about. I wonder if he happened to see an unoccupied tent pitched somewhere within a quarter of a mile of his house one day last summer. . . ?"

3

"You again?" asked Gudgeon, after opening the top half of his front door. "I find greeting you courteously twice within twenty-four hours a severe strain on my social behaviour. I mean it's not the most pleasant of things to have the cop that arrested me virtually camping out on my doorstep."

Masters said: "I've brought along a friend and colleague of mine to meet you."

"To meet me, or get a good look at me for future reference?"

"To meet you and to ask you a question."

"What question?"

Green said: "It would be warmer talking in the Battery Office, Major."

"Battery Office?"

"Sorry. Company Office. I was a gunner myself and so Battery comes naturally whereas Company is a bit foreign to me."

Gudgeon bent over to unbolt the bottom half of the door. It had been obvious that his upper garment was heavy-knit, roll-neck, dark-blue sweater such as a fisherman might wear. When he opened the lower half he showed that the rest of his visible apparel consisted of carefully creased, very pale grey slacks and highly polished brown shoes of good weight and substance.

"Come in," he ordered, rather than invited. "I'd better hear your question, though what the hell Scotland Yard wants to talk to me about is something more than I can begin to guess." He bent to bolt the bottom half of the door. "My daily help has gone, otherwise I wouldn't let you over the doorstep." He closed the top half of the door. "Let somebody like her get wind of the fact that I had been visited by a couple of rozzers and my reputation would be gone. Seriously, I'd have been obliged to leave this cottage. You may find that hard to believe. But we aren't used to constabulary activity round here. The biggest crime in Yourhead last year was a lad riding a bike without lights."

"Don't you believe it, chum," said Green.

Gudgeon stared hard at him. They were standing very close together in the minute hall. "The attention you are paying me argues that you think I am implicated. Masters should know better. He is well aware that I only amuse myself by killing people, not by getting up to other forms of devilry."

"Don't be bitter," counselled Green. "Not anymore. As an army officer you should know that life can be a hell of a minefield. You were unlucky enough to tread on two anti-personnel jobs in quick succession. Others manage to escape them all. But at least you have the satisfaction of knowing that if you were kicked hard in the crutch on both occasions, the explosions carried off two very nasty villains for all time."

Gudgeon continued to stare at him, and then suddenly grinned. "D'you know, Mr Green, I think you've got something of a philosophical point there. One which had escaped me, I must admit. But there, philosophical points of view are hard to take when one is in agony after . . . well, when one is having to hold one's crutch to ease the pain after two hard kicks in so sensitive an area."

"That's the ticket, Major. There's a poem I'm very fond of. I don't know whether you've heard it, but the first line goes: 'Oh, yesterday the cutting edge drank thirstily and deep.' Then it goes on to describe the wounded and the hacked, disfigured dead. Then the last line says: 'But tomorrow, by the living God, we'll try the game again.'"

Gudgeon turned to Masters, a yard behind them. "A poetry lover as well as a philosopher. I might get to like your colleague, Chief Superintendent."

"He has his points," replied Masters, "and as good a fund of earthy commonsense as you could meet in a month of Sundays."

"In that case. . . ." Gudgeon led the way into his gleaming sitting-room. "If you're proposing to stay, take your coats off and put them on the settle."

When they were seated round the driftwood fire, Gudgeon said: "Right. Let's have it. What's the question you came to ask?"

Masters said: "You told me last night that you get up pretty early, particularly in the decent summer weather, and walk along the front for exercise."

Gudgeon nodded. "I do it in the winter, too. I collect lumps of wood that get thrown up on the beach. I'm burning some of it now. Not a crime is it?"

Green said: "I reckon you should stop thinking we suspect you of any crime, Major. We don't. At least, we know nothing against you, and so the purpose of our visit is not to nick you for gathering flotsam or jetsam, or whatever planks of wood are."

"I'm pleased to hear it. But what's all this about my early morning movements—if you'll pardon the expression?"

"We are looking for a man whom we believe to have been abducted by a crowd of villains," said Masters.

"From here? In Yourhead?"

"We have reason to believe so."

"That's not the sort of caper that goes on round here, as I've told you."

"Nevertheless, our man was on a camping holiday. Or rather, he was on a naturalist's safari, moving around sleeping in a tent. We think he came this way. The vital dates are September the third and fourth, or so we believe. But in any case his trip was during the first fortnight of September."

"Go on," said Gudgeon quickly.

"As far as we can make out he pitched camp some-where here, near Barway Cliff, obviously intending to spend the night in his tent. My belief is that he was taken that night from his tent, which was left for the whole of the next day, to disappear that second night."

"Name of Hopcraft by any chance?" asked Gudgeon.

Masters nodded. "Arthur Hopcraft. How did you come to know his name? Was he a friend of yours? Did you meet him, perhaps?"

"Neither of those," replied Gudgeon. "But I think I'd better tell you in my own way."

"Please do. In as great detail as possible."

Before complying Gudgeon got to his feet and crossed the room to a desk. From the top drawer, he took a navy-blue, hardback book. "I keep a diary," he said. "This is last year's." As he sat down, he opened it and sought the page he wanted. "September the fourth. Unoccupied tent erected on Barway Cliff Lawn."

"Lawn?" queried Green.

Gudgeon looked up. "It is known as the Lawn," he replied. "And a very good name, too. I don't know whether you've been along the front past the lifeboat station?"

"Yes," replied Masters. "Only as far as the place where you can turn a car."

"Ah, yes, but if you were busy talking you wouldn't notice the Lawn. Quay Street goes on past the pub and the gasworks and turns slightly so that you can't get a proper view. But in these past few years the local council has improved things along there. Basically, they've made room for car-parking on both sides, put in public lava-tories and a couple of a more modern type of shelter. Beyond that they've made the turning circle for cars with a decent flowerbed in the middle of it. That is the end of the road and the beginning of the Lawn. You ought to have noticed all that.

"They have erected a fence at this near end of the Lawn. Quite a pleasant one that doesn't obtrude at all, and they've put a farm-type gate in it for getting the grass mowers in, as well as a kissing-gate for pedestrians. Once through the latter you are on to a tarmac path just wide enough to take two persons abreast or, more usually, some old dear with her dog on the lead. This path runs straight as a die the length of the Lawn. It is on the seaward side and the distance between it and the edge of the miniature cliffs varies from just a few feet to several yards because, as you will appreciate, the coastline wavers about a bit. I've called them miniature cliffs, because that is what they are. A moderately active small boy could jump them easily, though he would be ill-advised to do so because there is no sand at all just there. The beach is pebbles. Not small ones. Biggish ones, all rounded and smooth due to the tide's action, but varying in size from a breakfast bap up to the size of a small cottage loaf. Here and there, at the easier points, people have worn little paths down to the stones, and there are those who, liking a fair amount of solitude, manage to put up deckchairs and to keep them despite the nature of the ground.

"The area between the path and the sea, just the strip that varies in width, is given over to its natural wild plants. None of the gardeners ever cuts or hoes there. The Lawn is different. You might be surprised to hear that it is a vast area of virtually level grassland. About six hundred yards long by two hundred wide, I'd say. And in both directions it runs into Barway Cliff. The left-hand side of the grass runs up to the almost vertical cliff you probably saw from the landward end of the quay. The path runs towards the face of the cliff that turns at right angles out towards the sea. Just at that point the cliff is not quite so sheer. It is still steep, but a little beaten track winds up between the trees, whose roots cross the way and form the risers for miniature steps. . . ."

"Lying bare, with the bark scuffed off?" asked Green.

"That's it. You can obviously envisage what I mean. Now, gentlemen, though the strip between the path and the sea is left severely alone, for the bushes and flowers to grow and to act as a haven for butterflies, moths and the like, the Lawn is mown from time to time. As I told you, there is a wide gate in the fence to admit the local council's gang mower. The grass is never shaved, neither is it allowed to grow knee-high. It is kept at a depth that provides a nice springy, spongey surface for toddlers to play on. There are no ball games allowed, so young mothers can take their prams there, spread their rugs and allow the nippers to crawl about."

Gudgeon looked up at Masters and Green who were plainly a little bemused by this long description. The Major laughed at their expressions. "You asked for everything in great detail."

Masters nodded.

"But don't think I'm playing you up. There is a reason for what I've been saying."

"I guessed there might be."

"You will have gathered that the Barway Lawn is pretty jealously guarded, without in any way impeding access to it or the quiet freedom of its use. On the right, the sea and stony beach form a fairly protective barrier except for the most agile of pedestrians, and the cliff to the left . . . well, I've been highly trained in the scaling of cliffs and buildings, but getting up or down by that route would make me think twice. The thousands of trees and the undergrowth would be more of a hindrance than a help to a mountaineer. How the devil that forest clings there defeats me. Certainly if one wanted to hide a body and could get it thirty or forty feet up and hide it among the bushes and tree trunks, it would be most difficult to discover. For police to comb it thoroughly would be next to impossible, and certainly dogs could not work there."

"Are you suggesting," asked Masters, "that Hopcraft's body could be hidden there?"

"Offering it as a possibility. Not a probability, because I cannot for the life of me see how a dead body could be hauled up without employing a number of men equipped with lifting tackle to do the job. And certainly not an exercise one could easily conceal."

"Would the same objections arise if one were to lower a body from the top of the cliff to hide it halfway down?"

Gudgeon considered this for a moment. "It could be done more easily," he said. "With a lowering rope, somebody to take the strain and somebody to guide the body through the trees and bushes. I've never tried to do it, but I should imagine an inert body would be very difficult to manoeuvre in circumstances like that, at night. So I'm not terribly happy about giving that way the nod, either."

"So what do you reckon?" asked Green.

"For one thing, I don't favour the idea of sending the body downwards because to begin with, you'd have to get it to the top in some way."

"I'm not following you," said Masters.

"I'd better continue with my story," replied Gudgeon, "and we can speculate later.

"I told you that the Lawn is fenced at this end. Slap alongside the kissing-gate, facing outwards, is a very large notice board which says, quite bluntly, NO CAMPING. On September the fourth, a beautiful day, incidentally, I was up before half past five and walking along a totally deserted sea front.

"I walked past the lifeboat station and the turning circle in the road, before going through the gate to the Lawn. I was very surprised to see a tent pitched not above a dozen yards behind the notice board forbidding camping."

"Ah!" said Masters. Green shifted in his chair. In the minds of both men was the thought that here, at last, was a witness with solid facts to impart.

"I went across to the tent," continued Gudgeon, "because I could see that the flap was wide open, and I thought I could look in and tell the occupant that in his own best interests he should crawl out of his sleeping bag and strike his tent before the local beat man appeared. I thought that at least it would save some un-pleasantness.

"But I regret to tell you, gentlemen, that the tent was unoccupied. There was a bedding roll inside and one or two other bits and pieces strewn about on the ground-sheet, but no sign of the camper himself. I told you that some new public lavatories have been built near the parking areas, so I imagined our friend had gone there and would shortly return. So I hung about. Actually, I was very interested in his tent. It was a two-man ridge bivouac, olive-green in colour. But what interested me most about it was the side nearer the sea. I'd never seen one of that particular pattern before. Running diagonally across the slope, from top right to bottom left, was a heavy-duty zip-fastener. This was protected from rain by a flap, a couple of inches wide, which was sewn all along the top edge of the zip and just naturally fell over the mechanical part, like the eaves of a roof, to keep the water from soaking through the enmeshed teeth.

"The purpose was easy to understand. That side of the tent was double skinned, and the zipped area took clothes—either to get them out of the tent space but still keep them dry at night or, after the tent had been struck and carefully folded on the ground with that side up-permost, to use the two triangular pockets as a valise for bedding and clothing. When the tent was rolled up, everything would be in the one bundle for backpacking. Quite ingenious, actually, but how practical I wouldn't like to say before trying it out.

"I spent some time taking all this in, gentlemen, but still the camper didn't return. Eventually I continued my walk to the end of the Lawn, expecting perhaps to meet the chap on the return journey."

"No luck?" asked Green.

"None. And by then there was a Panda car on the turning circle and a young constable looking around. If you were to walk along there by night you would see that the turning circle is very well lit with those yellow lights—sodium, are they called? The point of my mentioning that is that our camper, even if he arrived after dark—which I feel he must have done, otherwise late-night dog-walkers would have put him right—could not have failed to see the NO CAMPING notice as he went through the gate on to the Lawn. I may be wrong, but I think even the most anti-authority character would not have flouted the warning quite so flagrantly. I think they would have crossed the grass to pitch under the cliff, or else continued along the path to get to the furthermost point, and thus be virtually out of sight."

"There's something in what you say," agreed Masters, "and our more anti-authority brethren are not often to be found among the ranks of the hikers and campers in my experience. So what are you saying, Major? That Hopcraft came down the little path with the tree roots for stairs at the far end of the Lawn?"

"I believe so. I think he then came along the path and when he got close to the near end, realized that good camping ground was giving way to roads and buildings. So, as it was late, he pitched his tent, not realizing that a dozen yards away was a board forbidding him to do just that."

"Logical," agreed Green.

"I think so," said Gudgeon. "Of course, I'd heard nothing of abduction until this morning. But abduction of a grown man—presumably a fit one, too, if he was a hiker—is not the sort of thing that can be done on the spur of the moment. I envisage it as a planned operation. And to plan an operation of that sort, the abductors would have to be aware of Hopcraft's movements. If they were aware of them, it would have been far easier to take him at the top of the cliff, or just as he started down, unsure of his footing and laden with tent and baggage. But not only easier to take, gentlemen, also easier to dispose of if they intended to kill him. From up top, he could have been lowered into obscurity. From down below he could not have been lifted to it nearly so easily."

Masters looked at his watch. "I am totally absorbed in what you are telling us, Major, but it is a quarter to twelve now and I am expecting a colleague at the hotel. . . ."

"I don't want to hold you up, but there's quite a lot more."

"I guessed as much. You haven't yet touched upon how you knew his name was Hopcraft. Unless it was printed on the tent."

"No. No that. Give me another few minutes, Masters. . . ."

"Of course. Please go on."

"I made it my business to be out and about several times that day. I was interested to see what happened to the tent, and what sort of a chap it was that would leave his belongings unguarded in that way. The policeman came along there once or twice, too. He was an understanding lad. He didn't want to strike the tent and cart everything off if it could be avoided. All he wanted was to give the owner a rocket and, at worst, some sort of summons that would result in a five quid fine. But nobody came. The bobby did say that it began to look as though the owner had gone missing and was probably in the hospital or lying somewhere with a broken leg. Finally he decided that if the chap hadn't turned up by the next day he would have to start some sort of enquiry.

"I was up again very early the next morning and, inevitably, went along to look at the tent." He shrugged his shoulders. "It wasn't there, gentlemen. All had been packed up and taken away. I assumed the owner had returned, realized he'd made a bloomer by camping there, and so had made good his escape during the hours of darkness, thereby avoiding any possible confrontation with the police. The only alternative which occurred to me was that the police had finally decided to impound the stuff after reading the young constable's daily report.

"However, I walked over to where the tent had been standing. I told you the grass was four or five inches high. There, I found a pocket notebook. Whoever had taken the gear had missed it in the dark." Gudgeon got to his feet and again crossed to the desk. From the same drawer he took a black, hardcover notebook with a red spine. It measured about six inches by four and was a good half-inch thick. He handed it to Masters.

Masters opened the front cover. "A. Hopcraft," he said. "So that's where you got the name from."

Gudgeon nodded as he sat down. "If you examine it, you will see all sorts of nature notes and little drawings. I read it with some pleasure and then decided not to hand it to the police."

"Why was that?"

"I thought that if the chap had managed to get away unseen it seemed a pity to give his identity to the police."

"It didn't occur to you that the man might be hurt or in some danger?"

"Frankly, no. I inclined to the view that he'd come back, rolled up his tent and stole away, as the Bible has it. That argued against him being any sort of casualty. And anyway, if the police had taken his gear, he'd have had to apply to them to get it back, so he'd have given them his name in any case."

"Thank you very much, Major Gudgeon." Masters got to his feet. "May I ask just one more question?"

"Fire away."

"How do you find life here?"

"Pretty tepid. Oh, I amuse myself and keep fit, but I confess I miss service life. I've never told anybody else that, but it's true. One can't just cut off the past—not the good parts, anyway."

Green, seeming to divine Masters' thoughts, asked: "You'd like to be in harness again?"

"Most certainly."

"No matter for how short a time?" asked Masters.

"What are you getting at?" asked Gudgeon suspiciously.

"A job as acting, unpaid lance-corporal," grunted Green.

"I don't understand."

"We are on a job that we don't wish to discuss with all and sundry," replied Masters. "So we're a bit short on talent—especially local talent. But we've had to show some of our hand to you. In other words you are inextricably linked with what we're about. As you are so involved—as what you have told us makes you—I would rather have you on the inside than the outside where you might get too inquisitive without the restraints that being a member of our team would place upon you."

"Go on."

"If you would care to help us, I should brief you just as much as it would be wise for me to do so. You would know the problem and help us to solve it. I can make no promises that it would be other than unexciting, dreary perhaps, but at least it would be a temporary return to service life of a sort."

"I'll buy it," replied Gudgeon quietly.

"Then in that case, why not come along with us now to the Water's Edge? We'll have a drink and a sandwich lunch, and a full conference this afternoon."

"Done," said Gudgeon. "While you get your coats on, I'll fetch one for myself."

DCS Pollock had driven himself from Truro and had reached the Water's Edge before midday. As he was signing in, Berger had appeared in Reception.

"Good morning, sir. Mr Masters is out with Mr Green at the moment, but he asked me to meet you. They haven't a day-porter here at this time of the year, so would you like me to take your bag up to your room?"

"That's nice of you, son. Sergeant Berger, isn't it?"

"Yes, sir."

"It's nearly two years since I saw you, but it's good to meet you again."

"Thank you, sir. What room number?"

Pollock looked at the large red tag on the key. "Fifteen."

"Right alongside the DCI then. This way, sir."

Berger led the way to the stairs and negotiated the fire doors and turns in the landings leading to the room.

"Here you are, sir. Mr Masters shouldn't be long, so if you'll look in at the residents' bar, between the dining-room and the lounge. . . ."

"Come in," invited Pollock as he unlocked the door. "I gather we couldn't say anything downstairs, but what's all this about?" He closed the door behind them and hefted his case on to the slatted stand.

"Actually, sir, I know very little. Until yesterday morning, when we drove down here, none of us even knew the DCS was on a case. But it appears he's been beavering away on his own for several months."

"Like that, is it?"

"Very secret, sir, but there's to be a conference this afternoon, so you'll get to know what it's all about then. Meanwhile, we've got a cover story for being here. We're a police commission set up to look into and discuss the merits of special squads in each seaside area to combat the rowdies who descend on resorts and break them up. We just happen to have chosen Yourhead as a meeting place."

"I see. So if anybody can overhear us we start talking loudly about gangs of skinheads on bikes."

"That's roughly it, sir. Mr Masters has forbidden any discussion of Operation Hosepipe in public rooms."

"Hosepipe. I know the code-name. It came in the warning order. Right, lad, I'll do a bit of unpacking and join you in the bar. P'raps I'll get Bill Green to buy me a drink. You never know."

"I wouldn't count on it, sir."

Berger had the bar to himself. He stood at the window gazing out at the still grey, though rapidly improving, day. From there he had a view along the esplanade in the direction of the harbour. He had been there a good ten minutes before he saw Masters and Green, accompanied by a stranger in a flat hat and fawn wind-cheater, walking towards him along the pavement opposite the promenade.

"Not drinking, son?" asked Pollock, behind him.

"I don't like drinking alone, sir."

"Have one with me, then."

"The other two are coming, but they've got somebody in tow."

"Who?" asked Pollock, looking through the window.

"I don't know him, but I suspect he's a chap called Gudgeon. An ex-army major. That's who Mr Masters went off to see."

"Is he connected with you-know-what?"

"I reckon he must be, sir. But beyond that I can't say."

"Right, son, I'll line them up. Does your DCS drink beer? Last time I worked with him he wasn't allowed alcohol."

"He takes a drink again now, sir."

The reunion was loud and cheerful. It pleased Masters to see how delighted Pollock appeared to be at meeting them all again and—at a guess—being called out to help with some secret case which could conceivably get him out from behind his desk for a few days.

"This is Major Gudgeon. He lives locally. He and I have met before, so it seemed a good idea to bring him along for a drink and a bite."

"Pleased to meet you, Major," said Pollock. "What unit? Infantry? Commando?"

"Infantry," admitted Gudgeon.

"Don't let him fool you, Fred," said Green to Pollock. "He answers to the name of Charles, by the way, and when he says he was an infanteer, so he was. At least that was his parent unit. But he did a good long stint in the SAS, actually. Fit as a flea, he is."

"You went from the PBI to the SAS?" asked Pollock.

"And back again."

"Why? I mean how does that come about?"

"You join the army and then, if you're the bloke they want and you're prepared to go, they second you to the SAS—on attachment. I stayed with them for some years, then circumstances forced me out, back to my own battalion."

"Forced you out? Meaning what?"

"Nothing sinister. The SAS is a young man's game. By the time you get to thirty-four or so, you've got to get on to the planning side rather than the physical, if you get my meaning. I was a bit unlucky. When I got into that

83

age band and consequently the promotion zone, all the jobs I might have done were filled by officers not much older than myself. So there was no opening for me in the foreseeable future. I returned to my battalion on promotion to major. As a company commander."

"I see," said Pollock. "And now you're out, eh? Enjoying retirement."

"Not quite," replied Gudgeon quietly. "I was more or less kicked out."

"Really? What for?"

"Shooting a man in Northern Ireland. They court-martialled me."

"Cashiered?"

"Found not-guilty and no longer wanted."

"What bloody bad luck."

"That's not quite the end of the story, Mr Pollock. Your friend George Masters was obliged to arrest me for killing one of a pair of villains who had broken into my house and who, besides the theft and damage, were frightening the life out of my wife—literally."

Pollock stared at him for a moment. "If George Masters acknowledges you as a friend, it means he has no quarrel with what you did, and that's good enough for me."

"Thank you. But he sent me down for it."

"No," said Pollock, shaking his head. "He probably arrested you in the line of duty, but he didn't send you down. The court did that."

"You're right. Have another drink. Bitter, is it?"

Berger said to the whole company: "As we're the only ones in here, they're going to bring a trolley of food in. There'll be Welsh rarebit, pork pie and sandwiches with coffee later."

"Well done, lad," said Green. "Make sure they bring some mustard for the pork pie . . . oh, and some Worcester Sauce for the Welsh rabbit. I like mine to taste of something and there's no taste in cheese these days."

After having his coffee, Masters said to Pollock: "We're still waiting for two more. We'll go into full session when they arrive, but I'm going up to my room now. If you'd like to come with me I can give you some idea of what we're about before the meeting. I've got a suite with a sitting-room. We jaw in there."

"I'll come along, George. I'm burning with curiosity."

As he turned to go, Masters said to Green: "When the others arrive, give Dr Moller time to settle in and then bring everybody along, will you, Bill, please. Take your time, because I've got a lot to say to Fred."

"Right, George."

Masters spoke long and earnestly to Pollock, who interrupted with nothing more than a few whys and hows from time to time. He had covered most of the ground the others knew—with the exception of Gudgeon's contribution—by the time Green arrived with his three colleagues. While the introductions were being made, Dr Harry Moller, the Senior Scientific Officer, handed Masters a sealed envelope, unaddressed. "I was told to guard this with my life and hand it to you personally, George."

Masters accepted the package. "Thank you. If you'll excuse me, Harry, I'll read this straight away." Inside was another envelope addressed to Masters. The flimsy sheet inside took him very little time to read. Then he put it carefully into his inside pocket.

"Thank you, gentlemen. We have a lot to talk about. All of you are variously informed about Operation Hosepipe. Major Gudgeon the least so, but I feel sure he will soon get the drift of what we are discussing and can then supplement his knowledge with questions if the need arises.

"So that we know what is causing all the trouble, I am going to ask Dr Moller to tell us, in easy-to-understand, laymen's terms, something of the Rutland innovation, its importance and, possibly, its dangers." He turned to Moller. "Please don't be too technical, Harry. An idiot's guide is what we need."

Moller, a bright man in his middle thirties, with a lock of brown hair falling over his forehead, looked totally unlike the typical boffin. He had a face thin enough to show up a fine bone structure, eyes which seemed to find the world humorous, exquisitely manicured hands and a pleasant baritone voice that was, in itself, a pleasure to listen to.

"Because of the highly secret nature of this business," he began, "I have not been allowed to put one word about it on to paper. So not only have I no notes to help me, I have not been able to prepare flip charts to help you to understand.

"I feel sure most of you will have seen and heard something about the process I am going to describe. On television, perhaps, because biotechnology is no longer a new thing and the programme makers love telling the world at large of all the possibilities now open to us using these techniques.

"Let me use something that you all might recognize as an example. The diabetic. At its simplest, a diabetic is a human who can't produce enough insulin within himself to keep his body chemistry right. So he has to be given insulin by injection. The insulin comes from cows and pigs—from the pancreas of those animals, because it is the pancreas that produces insulin, in humans as well as animals.

"But human insulin is better than animal insulin for humans. Or let us say it is. Or perhaps let us say the supply from animals was in danger of drying up for some reason. So we would have to go elsewhere for the drugs to keep diabetics alive.

"In theory, we can do that now, by biotechnology. The pancreas is a nucleus of cells. Say we were to take out of a human pancreas one cell, and then take from that cell just one gene—one that is responsible for directing the cell to make insulin—and then graft that gene on to the chromosome of a bacterium. You all know what would happen. During its life cycle, that bacterium would produce exactly the same chemical as the human cell. In other words you would get human-type insulin being produced by bacteria.

"I suspect you all know that bacteria are so small as to be invisible to the naked eye. But they replicate so quickly, that from just one you can culture millions in a day, and then you can start to see them, in colonies. You've all seen photographs of colonies growing in laboratory dishes and, indeed, on bad food and vegetable matter.

"All this is the work of microbiologists such as Dr Hopcraft. But don't let me give you the impression that the work is simple. Far from it. For instance, after you've got the bacteria to produce your insulin, you are then faced with the problem of separating the chemical you want from the bacterial cell.

"Even that has been achieved with some chemicals and some bacteria, so the problem is capable of solution, and Rutland believe they have done it, not for insulin, of which we have been talking, but for the chemicals which will neutralize cancer cells.

"Now, gentlemen, in this operation the problems are vast and the secrets equally big. For instance, the bacteria to be used for the process: there are millions of the wretched things. Each of us has many in his body. We couldn't live without them. One of the most common in the human gut is *E. Coli* and I know that successful experiments using this technique have been carried out using *E. Coli* taken from a human being. But one of Rutland's closely guarded secrets is which particular organism they are using as the host for their gene transfer. That knowledge alone is worth more than one can express in terms of money and I will try to explain why."

Gudgeon held up a hand to signify he had a question. "I know very little about this sort of thing, but I did see a programme which stated that we could grow enough protein in this fashion to feed all the starving people in the world. Am I right?"

"Yes. Such protein has been produced. As yet, I believe, it is nothing more than fawn-coloured powder and not terribly exciting as food, but the necessary proteins are there once the plant to make the stuff in large enough quantities is available."

"Thank you."

"To return to Rutland. As you probably all realize, cancer is caused by a cell in the body going rogue. It grows and continues to grow, free of the control which guides the growth of normal cells. That means that the chromosomes in the cell are out of kilter. Those that should curtail the activity of the cancer-causing cells have changed or are too weak for their job, or alternatively, the cancer-causing cells themselves have—if you like—grown too powerful to be restrained by their normal controls." Moller looked around him. "That is a very simple and mechanical way of describing how cancer comes about. Please understand it is a very complex business and one which I am in no way qualified to expound in serious technical detail."

"We realize that," said Masters, "and I think we all understand what you are trying to convey."

"In that case, we'll push on. Dr Hopcraft, as you already know, was a young, but already eminent molecular biologist. Rutland would give me no precise description of his achievements, but they did inform me that he and his team believed that they had discovered that there are five changes in the chromosomes in cells causing cancer. They refused to tell me whether the five changes occurred in every chromosome or whether each chromosome could be affected by one of five possible changes. Personally I lean towards the view that each chromosome can be affected by one or all the changes.

"However, that I think doesn't concern us. Hopcraft believed he had to stop five changes—all of them, I suspect, quite simple chemical changes. So, having learned the chemical configuration of what goes wrong, Hopcraft and his colleagues had to attempt to synthesize ready-made chemicals which would readily pass into the affected cells and nullify the changes.

"The biotechnology I mentioned earlier provided the means of synthesizing the chemicals. That was a matter of finding the ideal bacteria and locking on to them the human genes that would combat the cancer-causing cells. Then, as I explained, there was the business of separating the necessary material from the bacteria.

"So far, so good. But then came another problem, that of getting the resultant chemicals to pass readily into the affected cells. Gentlemen, you will, no doubt, be surprised to hear that though the bacteria themselves are too small to be visible to the human eye, and consequently their new chromosomes are much smaller, the new materials of this description are too big to pass into human cells."

"Too big?" demanded Pollock, disbelievingly. "You said those bacteria were in everybody's gut."

"Oh yes. In the tubes and intestines and waste matter—urine always contains them, for example—but not within the cells. They can cling on to the outside of the cells and set up all sorts of nasties like inflammation and pain. In fact if the number of bacteria in urine gets too high, one gets cystitis or even—in severe cases— liver damage." He scratched his head for a moment in thought. "I wonder how I can explain that point. Ah, yes. This isn't an exact parallel, of course, but if you were to take a dry brick and put it in a bucket of water, the brick would soak up a great deal of the liquid. But the water would soak in between the little grains of sand or other ruck dust of which the brick clay is made. It would not actually enter the individual grains themselves."

"Understood," said Pollock. "Sorry to interrupt."

"Not at all. It's what we're here for. Anyway, the new synthesized chemicals—protein or ribonucleic acid chains or whatever they are—are too big to get into human cells. So, what to do about it?

"Remember Rutland says there are five chemical changes. I believe Hopcraft had somehow managed to chop those ribonucleic acid chains into five. When I say chop, please don't think I necessarily mean that they are literally cut up. They are probably separated out. The techniques involved in doing this are so high-powered and, obviously, unique to Rutland, that I cannot even begin to suggest how it is done. But I suppose you were all involved in the very simple matter of separating sugar from sand when you were little boys at school."

"Refresh our minds," said Pollock.

"A tablespoon of dry sand is mixed with a similar amount of granulated sugar. The job is now to separate them. There are hundreds of thousands of grains of one sort or another, so you obviously can't do it by hand. Then you remember that sugar dissolves in water, but sand doesn't. So you add a good deal of water to your mixture, stir it up well to dissolve all the sugar, and allow it to settle. You then pour off the liquid. The sand is left, while the liquid can be allowed to evaporate and that, in turn will leave sugar crystals. That, gentlemen, is a very simple experiment for children. Dr Hopcraft was faced with a much greater task: his was like building the Queen Mary as opposed to whittling out a toy boat with a penknife. And he had to do it in five different ways to isolate all the chemicals he needed. An immense task which has taken many first-class scientists ten or twelve years to perfect.

"That is the stage Rutland was at, gentlemen, when Hopcraft went missing. They had found the series of five compounds to reverse or neutralize the changes which cause cancer, and they had done a great deal of testing in human tissue culture, in living primates and pigs, which are, whether we like it or not, the nearest things to humans."

"Successfully?"

"Entirely successfully, according to Rutland. There is more trial work to be done, of course, as well as dose adjusting. But basically, the treatment will be a course of injections, given five at a time, over whatever period the trials show to be the right one."

"Five jabs at once?" asked Reed, in horror.

"Nasty, perhaps, but better than cancer."

Nobody commented on this. After a short pause,

Moller went on: "Those are the secrets that are so important, gentlemen, and which have been stolen by the abduction of Dr Hopcraft because he has everything in his head. His abduction and the theft are serious crimes in themselves. But with secrets of this magnitude, the theft is probably the greatest ever. Not one of us here can visualize the wealth potential if what I have told you is used unscrupulously. Nor can we imagine the social blackmail which can be perpetrated on sick people or the consequent political upheaval all this could cause.

"I feel sure DCS Masters has mentioned these matters to you, but I would like to add just a few thoughts so that nobody is left in any doubt as to why we must tread warily and bring this affair to a successful conclusion.

"Cancer is a highly emotive subject. Across the world, millions of people consider they are under sentence of death because of it. Because of this, once the news leaks out that a cure exists, there will be a tidal wave that no government will be able to stem. People who have weeks, or at the most, months, to live will not be prepared to let national Drug Commissions spend time testing for safety and side effects, quibbling about data sheets and so forth. They will demand instant treatment. And I mean demand, gentlemen. And who will be the only people capable of meeting that demand? The people who have Hopcraft. They will have produced their bulk supplies in readiness for their announcement, which will, of course, be made at a time of their own choosing."

"Hold it a moment," growled Green. "Why shouldn't we produce it, even without Hopcraft. I know there's nothing in writing, but the bench diaries will have been kept by Rutland."

"People are wary of announcing wonder drugs in this country. What do you say? Have a television announcer say, 'Doctors and scientists in this country believe they might have discovered a cure for cancer. Full results of tests and trials may be available in two or three years' time.' That sort of thing? We've heard it all before. Everything in the conditional tense—may, might perhaps.

91

Then Rutland would have to take out the patent and everybody in the world would jump on it."

"George said the Libyans could be entering patents."

"George may be right, but I don't think so. And I'll tell you why. I don't think the Libyans will let anybody else get a sniff of this drug. It will be made and used exclusively in Libya."

"That's rubbish," said Pollock.

"Is it? What if they were to set up a row of dirty great clinics with a score or so Nightingale wards in each? Each ward with thirty beds? Easy enough to do in Libya. Space is no problem. They'd just lay out the wards like army huts on the nice, warm desert sand. And then they'd invite people in for the cure at whatever price they saw fit to charge for a fortnight's stay and a course of jabs. Think of it! The kudos to be got as the healing centre of the world! And the trade! It would beat your Costa del Sol and Greek Islands. It would beat all the holiday centres rolled into one, because most of the patients wouldn't go there unaccompanied. Parents, spouses, children would flock in with their loved ones, to stay in huge hotels rushed up for the job. Money galore! Money galore to make up for the money not being made by the failing Libyan oil industry. And nobody getting their hands on samples of the drug nor sight of the formula and processes in the patent. Oh, yes, Rutland could squawk that the innovation was theirs, but would it matter? And they could try to register their patent when they're ready to go. But I'll bet Gadaffi has a pair of eyes somewhere in this country, watching to see when that patent is to go in. His will be ready and will beat it by just the time necessary to do all that has to be done to get the thing signed, sealed and delivered. You're right. The cat will then be out of the bag, but all the licensed manufacturers will have to pay Libya for the right to produce the stuff, not Rutland. And the operation near Tripoli? It will go on. Probably at a lesser rate, but the facilities will be there. Eventually the business will die down, but Libya will have gained a lot and lost nothing but a few hundred army huts and a score of rubbishy hotels which it can turn into flats for homeless bedouin." Moller sighed. "And then there's the political angle. We know which blocs would say they didn't believe us. But what about a lot of our so-called friends? How many would go along with us if there were money and good health at stake by doing so? Because, my friends, once the patent is out, bulk production would not start in other countries in a few days. The operation is tricky, and requires specialist equipment. Factories to produce the stuff could take a long time to build, and so others would still be dependent on Libya."

"So they're laughing all the way, are they?" growled Green.

"I think they could be."

"And you reckon they could do all this even though they've only got Hopcraft."

"They've only got one Hopcraft," admitted Moller. "But don't run away with the idea that they'll be short on good brains to back him up. The Libyans have got scientists training everywhere, even in our own universities; in the States, Moscow, Japan and Vienna, and also in Alexandria and Cairo which have some good educational establishments. They're being trained now, but—as we know for a fact—they have quite a band of nationalistically minded scientists already in being. Those that had the oil scholarships and the like in the past two decades."

"You're supposing that Hopcraft is co-operating with them?"

"No. Or at least he's not doing so willingly. But everybody here knows what things a man can be forced to do against his will. Refined persuasion can be very successful against even the most obdurate of men. And I don't suppose Hopcraft has ever been taught to resist the tricks, the druggings and the long interrogations that trained thugs use relentlessly on their victims."

There was a moment or two of silence, then Masters

said: "There should be a tea trolley coming up anytime now. I suggest we take a break so as not to be caught in serious conference."

Pollock got to his feet and stretched. "How long are you going on for, George?"

"I'd like a session after tea. We'll break in good time for dinner, and I shall reserve an hour or so for meeting after that if necessary. Was there some reason for your question, Fred?"

"Not specifically. I just wondered whether you could fit in another personal talk with me. You've put me in the picture for the most part, but there are still a few bits and pieces I'd like to catch up on."

"I'll bear it in mind and we'll meet at the first opportunity. If the weather continues to improve we might get half an hour to walk along the esplanade together."

"Fair enough. Now, where's that tea you promised us? I'm feeling dry."

As soon as the tea was finished and the trolley put outside in the corridor by Berger, Masters said: "We have with us Major Gudgeon who has provided us with not only the information that shows we are on the spot, as it were, but also the one piece of material fact that we have. DCI Green and I have heard Major Gudgeon's story, but as you others are in the dark about it, I am going to ask him to repeat it, briefly, to bring you up to date. Major, perhaps you would make your report."

Gudgeon did as he had been asked. The others listened in silence to a concise account of how the empty tent had stayed on the Lawn for twenty-four hours. When the Major had finished speaking, Masters said: "Comments and questions, please gentlemen."

Pollock said: "It stands out a mile, George, that the villains knew exactly where Hopcraft was going to be and at what time. The Major said, and I agree with him, that it would have been far easier to knock him off on the little tortuous path which comes down off the cliff on to the Lawn. Therefore, I reckon they knew exactly where they wanted to take him."

Green grunted his approval of this.

Pollock continued. "So I reckon he was lured to the very spot. In other words, that girl, Eissa Al Something-or-other, said she would meet him there."

"That sounds not only logical, Fred, but very probable. Are you going to develop the theory for us?"

"With pleasure. I reckon he wouldn't have waited until dark before pitching camp unless he had an assignation with the girl at that exact spot. That means he would have spent the night somewhere up on the cliff top a mile or two back. In other words, I don't think he lit on that pitch by chance."

"Go on."

"They wanted him there—just a dozen yards behind the fence at this end of the Lawn. And I think they wanted him there, at that exact spot, because it is the last possible place to pitch a tent—legally or otherwise—within spitting distance of the harbour and the quay."

"Meaning that after they had abducted him they would have no great distance to carry him to a boat?" asked Gudgeon.

"Just that."

"You're right. There are hidden paths round the seaward side of the gas works and the pub—even round the lifeboat house—which could get them on to the quay at a point beyond the shelter and the kiosks there. They are unlit, just earth-trodden ways, and unlikely to be used after dark, even by young couples, because there are more attractive places for that sort of thing."

"How far along the well-lit front from the place where the tent was to the point where they could take to these unlit paths?" asked Masters.

"A hundred yards," replied Gudgeon, "but I think Mr Pollock is definitely on the right track."

"I'll ask you to expand that in a moment, Major. Fred, you were giving us your theory. Would you like to finish it in the light of the support for it that Charles has just given you."

Pollock nodded. "This is how I envisage it, George. You said that just outside the fence of the Lawn is the traffic turning circle and just before the road reaches the circle are small car-parks on both sides. I reckon the girl was parked there, watching and waiting for Hopcraft." He turned to Gudgeon. "The Lawn path, I take it, is unlit?"

"Totally. And though the car park to the right of the road is well-lit—it's just a space for a rank of cars to nose in to the side under the street lighting—the park to the left is ill-lit. It's a smallish square for a couple of dozen cars. Cut out of the rock of the cliff face, actually. That's where the lavatories are."

"Thanks. So this Eissa dame is watching for Hopcraft to come. She's in a car probably forty or fifty yards from the end of the Lawn, looking for a chap coming along an unlit path. She wouldn't spot him until he was getting fairly close to the fence. . . ."

"Good point," growled Green.

". . . so she'd run to meet him, and get him a few yards before he got to the kissing-gate. Then she suggested he should set up camp at that spot, a few yards from the path. He did that, and . . . well, as soon as the tent was up, her pals took him."

"Why wait until the tent was up?" asked Reed. "It would have been far better to take him and all his gear before it was unpacked, and would have saved the business of collecting it the next night, let alone arousing the speculation that was caused by leaving an unoccupied tent there for all the next day."

Pollock shrugged. "I can't answer that, Sergeant, except by falling back on the old saying that even the best-laid plans go wrong sometimes. Probably the heavy mob didn't get the signal soon enough or—and I think this is the most likely answer—there were people about. Late dog-walkers or a crowd of lads after the pub had turned out. People who would witness an assault and might wade in to help the victim. A bloke like the Major here, say, or somebody with an Alsatian dog. It probably held them up for ten or fifteen minutes."

Gudgeon said: "That's a good speculation, Mr Pollock. But if I could just add a thought. . . ?"

"Fire away."

"Had there been people close by, I think they would have warned Hopcraft about the 'no camping' regulation. In which case, the tent would not have gone up. But remember I said the lavatories were in the small square car-park to the left of the road. I think the girl, Eissa Al Barcurata, would have wanted to get Hopcraft to go there."

"Why?"

"Because the lavatories are straight opposite the place where those unfrequented paths I mentioned leave the esplanade. If they nobbled him in the loo, they'd only got to get him across a fairly narrow road, then they'd be out of sight. I think the yobs waited by the gents, while the girl had instructions to point him in that direction." Gudgeon shrugged. "It would be a natural thing for her to say. 'If you want to go to the loo it's just over there. And there's a basin where you can wash!' His reply, equally natural. 'Thanks. I'll just get the tent up, then I'll feel like a wash and a leak before bedding down'. So up goes the tent, and the girl says, 'Off you go. I'll be ready and waiting by the time you get back.' "

"I like it," murmured Masters. "It is an absolute certainty that he would want to visit the lavatory before going to bed. But he wouldn't know there was one handy, so presumably he was told of its existence—if he used it. But it also explains why, if he did go to the lavatory, he didn't see the NO CAMPING sign at the gate on his return. Charles said nobody could have missed it, and I suspect Hopcraft, had he seen it, would have obeyed the order. Therefore, one can assume he didn't see the board, which in turn could mean he was taken up at the lavatory building and then spirited across the road and down the quay to a waiting boat."

"It seems very feasible," conceded Green. "At any rate it takes care of everybody's objections." He turned to Gudgeon. "Just to complete the picture, Chas, can you remember if the tide would be in to float a boat in the harbour that night?"

"I'll have to look that up. But if it was in, all the thugs would have to do, after they'd arrived at the quay, is to hurry Hopcraft across it and down the steps to a boat. As opposed to carting him along the couple of hundred yards of its length, I mean."

"Will you consult your tide-tables and get us that information, please, Charles?"

"Of course."

"My last point," said Pollock, "is the fact that Hopcraft was not taken on the cliff footpath but was allowed to get as far as the spot where he pitched his tent argues that he is alive. That they didn't want to kill him, I mean, otherwise he'd have been knocked off earlier."

"I think that is right," agreed Masters. "At least we must hope so, because though our job is to find Hopcraft, alive or dead, and discover what happened to him, I would rather be looking for a live scientist than a corpse."

"Is there any chance that he could be dead, Chief?" asked Berger.

"I can only give you an opinion in answer to that. I believe Hopcraft to be alive at the moment, but that the closer we get to him, the greater his danger. By that I mean that those who have him need him alive to supply them with information, but that they will kill him rather than let us take him back. And that is one of the main reasons why our operation must be totally clandestine."

"There's a lot at stake," said Green.

"Have we the resources to do the job?" asked Gudgeon. "I mean this"—he spread his hands to indicate not only his companions, but also the room and their conference activities—"this may be high-powered, but it seems pretty small beer to me."

Masters grinned. "I would prefer the description low-key to small beer."

"What would you like to be doing, chum?" asked Green. "Planning an SAS raid to storm the captive's prison, wherever that may be."

"I should feel more at home were that the case," admitted Gudgeon.

"It may come to that," said Masters quietly.

They stared at him intently.

"You must have realized that possibility, Charles."

"Oh, yes. I'm not so big a fool as not to realize it. You have invited me to join your team. I don't flatter myself it was merely because I live hereabouts, or not entirely so. Had I not seen that tent that day, you could well have found some other excuse to invite me along. Since hearing what Dr Moller had to say, I believe I have sensed why you want me. Not to beat about the bush, you think Hopcraft may be in alien hands—held by the Libyans, perhaps in some remote desert spot. To get him out may require muscle. In other words, he may have to be fetched out by mounting a raid and snatching him back. But the trouble is that this country cannot mount an official raid in another state. So the muscle needed would have to be renegade muscle. Highly trained, but renegade, so that if the need arose—as it most certainly would—the government could officially deny all involvement in the operation. And you, looking ahead, have realized that I could be your man to plan such a raid, find the trained personnel for it, and perhaps even participate in the event."

There was a moment or two of silence.

"Any truth in what the Major has just said, George?" asked Pollock.

"Yes. Ever since I got to know that it was probably the Libyans who had abducted Hopcraft, I have been aware that his release might depend on a . . . well, our masters call it a counter-abduction. Should such an operation be needed in this country, all official resources, including

SAS, could and would be used. But as Charles has said, the matter is somewhat different in an alien state. That thought has been with me for weeks. When I saw the chance of co-opting the help of a professional in such affairs, I seized it." He turned to Gudgeon. "Nothing more than that, Charles. I want your help and advice on how to go about things. I am not expecting you personally to participate in an act of war. To that end, I felt it would be as well if you were put fully in the picture so that you would be in the best possible position to give me your advice. I could have got a currently serving officer, I suppose, at some time in the future. For better or worse I chose you, here and now. Partly because you are here, and partly because you are no stranger to me, as a currently serving officer would be."

Gudgeon grinned. "I'm not complaining."

"I didn't think you would be, which shows how right I was to enlist your help."

Pollock said: "This case gets curiouser and curiouser. As I might have known it would do with you involved, George. How strong is the likelihood of a raid becoming necessary? Charles here might be wanting to sharpen up his commando knife. . . ."

"I rate the chances as high," replied Masters. "But should it ever happen, serving police officers like you and me, Fred, would be out—were the raid on foreign territory, that is. However, you must realize that though we could not be present, the responsibility for such a raid would still be ours, just as if it were happening in this country and we had called for military assistance. Ours, Fred. Mine, obviously, and after that, yours, as the next senior officer. I dislike the idea of any business for which I am responsible going ahead in my absence."

"Me too."

"I have said I would not expect Charles to participate personally in a raid. I suspect he has different ideas. Should that be the case . . . well, at least we would have a member of this team on the spot and bearing, if I may put it so, our responsibilities for us."

Pollock turned to Gudgeon. "You heard the man, Major."

"Loud and clear, and I'm content to leave it there."

"Just like that?" asked Reed.

"Why not? To me it is only like the prospect of a new case would be to you. A job for which one has been trained."

Green said: "That's the stuff, Chas." He turned to Masters. "Fred asked what were the chances of us having to fish Hopcraft out of Libya. You rated them as high. I think so, too, but mine is only a gut feeling. Have you any more solid fact to go on?"

Masters grinned. "More solid than your gut, Bill?"

"Ha, ha!"

Masters was immediately serious again. "You all heard what Harry Moller had to say about the possibility of the Libyans building large hospitals so as not to let the substances out of their hands. That view is his own, but he is not the only one to hold it. Robby Lippert's friends consider it a distinct possibility, too, though they and Harry have never spoken together. Today you saw Harry give me an envelope he had brought down from London. It is from Robby who is, as it were, acting as liaison officer between his masters and us." He drew the envelope from his inside pocket. "I told Robby I was coming down here and that Harry would be joining us, so he used our friend as confidential messenger-boy to send me this letter. It says:

E.A.B. sighted leaving Homs for Zavigon Island aboard landing craft. Zavigon two miles out of Homs. Widely announced as being turned into holiday centre like islands in Sousse/Sfax area, Tunisia. Satellites appear to show one large central building well advanced. Radiating paths with rectangular foundations sited along both sides. Landing craft used for carrying materials and personnel."

He looked up.

"E.A.B. is, of course, Miss Barcurata, and I think one is entitled to wonder of what interest it would be to her to inspect a partly-built holiday complex."

"One large central building well advanced?" said Pollock. "With the ground floor completed and fitted out out as a laboratory and adjoining prison cell for Hopcraft?"

"That was my immediate thought on reading this message."

"I can't remember any offshore islands near Homs," said Green. "It must be pretty small. Nothing more than a sandbank showing above the water."

"All the better," said Gudgeon. "Easy to paddle ashore and land. I don't suppose we could find out if they guard new holiday centres with large bodies of troops, could we?"

"I think we could probably ask for that information," said Masters. "It should be fairly easy to come by if we can manage to keep an eye on Miss Barcurata."

"Ask for an aerial photograph," urged Gudgeon. "From an airliner flying over."

"Steady, chum," said Green. "They're fussy about the routes airliners fly out there. And where foreigners go."

"Of course. Sorry about that, Masters."

"I'll ask for full information. Meanwhile, perhaps you would give some thought as to how one might get people there—short of sending in the Royal Navy and the RAF with choppers."

"It will be an interesting exercise."

"Good. Now, gentlemen, I think we should break to get ready for dinner and to have a drink before we eat. Charles, I hope you will join us."

"I'd like to, but there are one or two things I must attend to. You hauled me out to come here at very short notice, you."

"Of course. But I should like us all to meet at nine o'clock. Would you mind turning out then to be here?"

"I've got a better idea. I can't invite you all to dinner for obvious reasons, but if you think a change of venue would be a good thing, why don't you all descend on me at nine o'clock. We can talk quite cosily there and have a noggin round the fire."

Masters looked round for signs of agreement or disagreement. Pollock spoke for them all. "Nice idea," he said. "If you'll let us bring a bottle, Major."

"No need for that, but thanks for the offer." He turned to Masters. "Could I make a suggestion?"

"Please do."

"Simply that you should drive past my place as far as the turning circle again and this time take note of the lie of the land for yourselves. A couple of minutes spent on viewing the lay-out might clarify a lot of what we've been talking about. You could leave your cars in the car-park near the lavatories and then walk the few yards back to my cottage. It would save giving away the fact that you are visiting me."

"We'll act on your suggestion," said Masters. "We may even walk. It's not all that far, the weather has improved a great deal and you probably heard Fred Pollock say he'd like to get out for a breath of fresh air."

"In that case, gentlemen, I'll see you at nine."

4

Soon after a quarter to nine, the six of them set off along the esplanade, walking in pairs. There was still a certain amount of wind, but now it was coming from the south-west and noticeably warmer. After their long stints in the hotel, they all welcomed the chance to be in the open air.

Reed and Berger were ten or a dozen yards ahead of Green and Moller. The chief superintendents were bringing up the rear.

Reed asked his companion: "Don't you reckon the Chief is trusting Gudgeon a bit too much?"

"On the face of it, I think he is. An ex-con being taken into his confidence on the biggest of the top-secret jobs he's ever had! It makes you think, that does, and the Chief has done it without reference upwards. If they were to get to know about it they'd blow their tops. And yet we both trust the Chief's judgement, and I must say that now I've met him, I think Gudgeon is a pretty sound bloke."

"Okay," said Reed. "But what about since we broke up before dinner? The Chief invited the Major to stay at the hotel. I'd have thought that invitation would have been accepted, because Gudgeon lives alone and he'll have had to cook his own supper. But he refuses, saying he's got this and that to do. The first thought that came into my head was that he heard a hell of a lot during the conference and that he couldn't wait to get to a telephone to let somebody know what he'd learnt."

"So you don't trust Gudgeon?"

"The funny thing is, I do—or think I do. But I couldn't help that thought coming into my mind. What I'm saying is, if this operation is so secret that the likes of you and me and Bill Green—to say nothing of Pollock—have been kept completely in the dark until now, isn't it a hell of a risk to let anybody else get even a whisper of what we're about, however trustworthy he is?"

"I get you. You're saying the Chief has made two glaring errors. One by involving Gudgeon and a second by allowing him to go off on his own to make what use he likes of his knowledge."

"Yes. Because yesterday the Chief was of the idea that one of the cottages along here had probably been, or was being, used by the villains as an operations centre. Now, bearing in mind the fact that when the Chief gets ideas they're usually somewhere near the mark, what do you think of his actions following the discovery that those selfsame cottages are actually housing an ex-con?"

"So you're saying the Chief's idea was at least half right, as shown by Gudgeon's presence, and yet he has now abandoned it in favour of this dicey business of trusting the ex-con he found on the very spot he was looking at."

"Right."

At this point the wide walk of the esplanade became the narrow pavement of Quay Street. So narrow that the sergeants had to walk in single file, and so conversation ceased.

Meanwhile, behind them, Green and Moller were discussing the case.

Green asked: "What do you reckon the chances are that this island holiday camp is really the big hospital you thought the Libyans would build?"

"I'm not entirely satisfied that it is a hospital or has any relevance to George's case."

"Even though the bit of capurtle was seen going there?"

"That could be just one of those things. If she is being spied on, she'll be seen in all sorts of places in Tripoli-

105

tania. She's obviously one of the government trusties out there and so could be involved in practically any undertaking in one way or another."

"But George was specifically sent that report. Robby Lippert thought it was relevant."

"Thought it *could* be relevant would be nearer the mark. I'll tell you why I'm sceptical, Bill. If the Libyans are bent on carrying out this treatment solely on their own territory, the island, as we've had it described to us, would be no earthly. Nor would one hospital such as you could get on it. They would need a huge complex, capable of being constantly and continuously enlarged. Square miles of it. As I said, it would be dead easy to build for the purpose for which it would be intended. And cheap, too. But even so, it would have to have services like water and sanitation, and they are not easily come by in Tripolitania. In other words they would have to be laid on, and it is a damn sight easier to build one sewage plant for a big complex than lots of little sewage plants for individual hospitals spread far and wide. Then there's the control of the drug—the making, the storing and the using. All dangerous points as far as the Libyans are concerned. Places where the stuff could be stolen for analysis. For security reasons, they'd want everything together. That's why I don't think that island is likely to be the hospital complex."

"I get your point. But couldn't it be the place where they're holding Hopcraft or where they're making the initial batches of the cure?"

"Where they're holding Hopcraft, perhaps. Indeed, one could argue that Eissa Al Barcurata's trip to the island was to see Hopcraft. To persuade him to do something he was bilking at, or . . . well, after all, she had been his mistress. It could be that she is still using her charms on Hopcraft. But manufacturing batches of the drug? I'd be inclined to doubt it. An island like that would have no supply of water of its own, for instance, and manufacturing anything without a constant water supply is virtually impossible."

"I get you, Doc. It all sounds convincing to me. But you don't entirely rule out the possibility of Chas Gudgeon getting his bit of fun by rescuing Hopcraft from there."

"Not entirely. Although the idea of his having to do that fills me with foreboding."

"Me, too. Hang on, Doc, it's pavement from now on. You go first."

Masters and Pollock were chatting, too.

Pollock said: "I don't have to tell you how pleased I am to be working with you, George. And I'm very chuffed to know you thought of me, so I'm not cribbing at all, but would you have had me on the team if you hadn't come down more or less to my part of the world?"

"Your name would always have been in the frame, Fred, but if I'd discovered I'd have to operate, say, in Newcastle, I'd have tried to find a replacement for you from up there. It seems commonsense, to me. But the number of the people I'd want is quite small, no matter where they come from. Not that I'm criticizing anybody's ability. That's not the only criterion. I obviously wanted an able man, but he had to be somebody I knew I could work with and who would, in turn, be prepared to work with my whole team. You know us all—with the exception of Moller and Gudgeon—you have some idea of how we go about things and you are prepared to accept our idiosyncratic way of working. It didn't take me a minute to decide to nominate you for this investigation."

"Thanks. Now one other thing, George. Why are you here, in this particular place? How did you get here? What decided you to come?"

"Lots of arrows pointed this way, Fred. I've been working on this alone and in great secrecy for some months now. I talked very closely to Hopcraft's colleagues. None could say exactly what his plans were except that he proposed to backpack his way around the countryside for a fortnight, which was a habit of his. He spent a couple of weeks doing so every year to keep his hand in as a naturalist, I believe. So that was no secret, but his destination was, or at least he didn't mention it.

"I went through his belongings. I found some of his old field notebooks. One was for this area—from a number of years back. I also found one of those little railway timetables: they are folded, measure about three inches by two, and carry train times for just one route. It was the one from Paddington to Penzance. There was a mark against the Saturday mid-morning train and another mark against its arrival time at Taunton.

"The thing was out of date, but the marks looked newish to me. I imagine he would have got a new one to carry with him."

"Reasonable assumption, I'd say."

"You've got to remember, Fred, that all these bits and pieces were reaching me in any old order. Nothing was chronological about them. But I did know, from his colleagues, that Hopcraft was finishing work on the Friday and proposing to start his holiday proper on the Saturday. I could get no sort of confirmation that he had caught that mid-morning train."

"Backpackers travel twenty to the dozen on Saturday mornings in summer."

"Quite. Now I don't know exactly when he'd disappeared. But when I heard about the girl being his mistress and her disappearance from Rutland, I had to theorize on their meeting up. Hopcraft's secrecy about his trip, and the broad hint he gave that it might not be entirely devoted to the study of plants, seemed to support the theory that they had met. There was every reason, I thought, to suppose they would meet up at the first possible moment. After all, there'd be no reason for the girl to absent herself from the office until she was just about due to meet him.

"So I assumed Hopcraft had reached Taunton at lunchtime on Saturday. I did the old trick of drawing circles on the map, centred on Taunton. I credited him with five miles on Saturday. Another eight on Sunday, and the same on Monday. The question was, where had the girl met him, and when?

"The Monday night line cut this coast north and south of Yourhead. I had one of Rutland's men go to the girl's digs and ask when she had clocked out. It was on the Monday morning, early, in her car, and she hadn't left a thing behind her. And when I say not a thing, I mean not even a scrap of paper. The landlady said she had noticed her lodger had visited the lavatory several times in quick succession the night before, so I assume she had flushed everything away."

"Suspicious, that," grunted Pollock.

"I thought it confirmed that she was implicated. Then, judging from the time of her departure, I decided that the earliest Hopcraft would have disappeared would be the Monday night. As I told you, I reckoned his travelling time would have taken him up to twenty or twenty-one miles from Taunton.

"I began to favour the coast more highly after I'd thought about the business of getting him away. Air seemed an unlikely way, sea a likely way. With the sea in mind I researched the Libyan mercantile marine— that was after I'd heard the girl was Libyan. I didn't even know Libya owned any ships, but if they had carted Hopcraft off by sea, they had to have mercantile contacts. Actually, I discovered they own two tramps and it was easy enough to discover that on their visits to this country they put into Bristol."

"Ah!" breathed Pollock. "They pass up and down the channel only a few miles from here."

"Just so. That—to my mind at any rate—seemed to justify my interest in the coast. So I asked all the local stations round here if they'd seen or heard anything of a camper that Monday night of September the third. At first the answer was a lemon and then somebody in Yourhead remembered a tent being left unoccupied the whole of one day. . . ."

"Bingo!" said Pollock.

"As I told you, Fred, there were lots of arrows pointing this way, but I had to discover them."

"I'll bet," said Pollock. "I know that business of getting

a hint here, half a hint there, one late fact before an early one and so on and so on. It's hard work at the time, George, no matter how easily it seems to fall into place after you've formed the right theory to fit what you know. You say it took you several months of private work and study. Lord knows how long it might have taken other folk. I take my hat off to you, George."

"Thank you, Fred."

"But I'd still like to know why we've forgathered here."

"Because the time had come when I felt I had to get my team together, and we had to meet somewhere. Somewhere where we were not so well known as to cause speculation. So why not Yourhead, the place where I believed Hopcraft to have disappeared? I'm a great believer in ambience, Fred. I can't really get the feel of a case when sitting at a desk at the Yard. The best place for me to be is at the scene of the action, even though the action is well over. There were two other reasons for being here. One to seek confirmation of my belief that Hopcraft was abducted here. . . ."

"Which we've plainly got after hearing the Major's report."

"That alone has been worth the visit. Now the second reason is. . . ."

"Let me guess," said Pollock. "If you're going to look for a man, the place to start is where he was last seen. So we are going to work from here to that end."

"Right. We'd be foolish not to do what we can around here."

"Will Gudgeon be useful?"

"I have high hopes of him."

"You trust him?"

"He's a man of principle. Stiff-necked and stubborn, some might call him. But he refused to confess a remorse he didn't feel after he killed the man who vandalized his home and frightened his wife to death. Had he done so, his sentence would have been cut by a year, maybe eighteen months. He knew that because I told him so myself, knowing that the judge whom he faced was the sort of man who was ready to accept an expression of remorse from a criminal at its face value, and take it into account when sentencing. Gudgeon scorned that course. His sense of responsibility is so great it is viewed nowadays as old-fashioned. But I'd trust him alongside me more than I would trust some police officers I could name."

"His life has been ruined, would you say?"

"If so, I think he is rebuilding it. He's far from wealthy. He made a bit, I imagine, by selling in London and buying down here. Probably just enough to fill out his pension to the point where he can afford the occasional bottle of whisky, but I don't think he has a car."

They, too, had by this time reached the point where the walk narrowed down to a scrap of pavement.

"Pier Head, George," said Green who had hung back to wait for Masters and Pollock. "Where you and I came this morning. There's the shelter and the kiosks"

"A row of shuttered Gifty Shoppies," said Pollock, "and then, from the looks of it, the Harbour Pub. You can see the unmetalled paths running down both sides. . . . Ah! The lifeboat house. Good cover behind all these buildings, George. And our old friend the gasometer. There always were plenty of blackspots round gas houses. Gudgeon was quite right about being able to operate in secrecy round here. The street lighting doesn't penetrate down these paths at all."

They moved on. The beginnings of a newer, wider pavement, with the white rectangles denoting car-parking spaces alongside it. Then a modern shelter, mostly glass. A few more yards and the pavement bent left as the road formed its turning circle round a central flowerbed. As they completed the semicircle of pavement, they caught up the remainder of the party, clustered at the kissing-gate.

"Big enough notice, Chief," said Reed, indicating the board which shone glassily under the lights. "Nobody coming this way could miss it."

Masters stared along the narrow path which ran away

into the darkness of the Lawn. "Almost eerie," he said to Green. "Such a huge area of almost total flatness—or so it seems, because one can't see all that far—and then that incredible cliff formation, rising perpendicularly and as black as night with its covering of trees."

"Cut it out," growled Green. "You're making me nervous."

They continued round the pavement of the turning circle, closing the foothill of the cliff as they did so.

"The car-park proper," said Pollock, just as the road began to straighten out. "Gudgeon said they'd dug it out, and so they have, but he didn't say it was double storied. See, George, there's a ramp up to a higher level."

"Ingenious," said Moller. "Ah! And here are the loos. Gents one end, the others the other." He disappeared for a moment. "Pretty good standard," he said on returning. "Few graffiti and a decent drinking-water tap where one could fill a kettle or bucket."

As soon as they were past the end of the car-park and a couple of old, padlocked sheds which seemed as though they could contain boating gear, probably for the lifeboat, they started to pass in front of the row of cottages, one of which belonged to Gudgeon.

He met them at the door and ushered them, almost one by one, into the tiniest of rooms on the right of the little hall, so that they could put their coats on the table and the two dining-chairs it was only just able to contain.

As they went across to the sitting room, Green handed Gudgeon a bottle of Bell's.

"I told you not to."

"Not me, you didn't. It was Fred Pollock you said that to."

"I meant everybody."

"The trouble with independent bastards like you, Chas," retorted Green, "is that you try to stop equally independent bastards like me from doing what they want to do."

Gudgeon grinned. "Thank you—for the whisky, not

the remark. And forgive me for forgetting the social graces."

"That's all right, chum. I don't expect life has treated you well enough these last few years to keep your social graces in good working order. But I suspect you've still got them all greased up in a state of heavy care and preservation, as we used to say of our mob store weapons."

"Quite right. Come and have a pew by the fire."

Gudgeon had prepared for their comfort by a little rearrangement of the furniture and the provision of a deck-chair for himself. When they'd all been supplied with a drink and the host himself was seated, Masters took charge of the meeting.

"We have established, to the satisfaction of everybody present, that Hopcraft was abducted from here, in Yourhead.

"We are, also as a body I believe, of the opinion that he is still alive. Does anybody disagree with that belief?"

"There's no absolute fact to support that opinion," said Pollock.

"But we have to accept it as a working basis. There would be no point in anybody snatching Hopcraft unless they wanted to learn what he knew, and that means keeping him alive so that it can be forced out of him. I would add, George, that we must also assume he is still alive, otherwise there is no point in our trying to find him."

"So we're turning an opinion into an assumption and an assumption into a fact, are we?" asked Green. He turned to Pollock. "I'm not disagreeing with you, Fred, but really and truly what we are after is not Hopcraft himself, but the formula he has in his head. What would happen to this operation, George, if Chas's phone were to ring to give you the news that Hopcraft was dead?"

"I honestly don't know the answer to that, Bill, but I am sure the operation would continue under some guise. As you said, it is Hopcraft's knowledge which is the jewelled eye of the toad. Our masters would still want us to discover whether the jewel had been removed from the body and, if so, to trace its whereabouts."

"So what are we saying?" demanded Pollock. "That we think he is alive, and proceed as if he were, while bearing in mind that he could be dead?"

"I think that is about it," admitted Masters. "My point in asking whether we were all of that opinion is lest somebody has some idea of how we should proceed to cover both contingencies rather than to investigate just the one possibility."

"You've raised a hare I didn't realize existed," said Moller.

"We must consider it," said Gudgeon. "Or, as a layman, I'd have said so. They've had Hopcraft for the best part of six months now. It's got to be a bloody good bloke who can hold out for six weeks under the pressure hit-men like the Libyans can bring to bear on the mind as well as the body. They could have sucked him dry and then finished him off long before this."

Moller replied: "While agreeing with everything Charles has said, I think there is one factor in our favour—and Hopcraft's—which is probably more evident to me as a scientist than to you other gentlemen.

"Hopcraft has probably been made to talk. But there is one thing his captors will have to be extremely careful about, and that is not to harm him too severely, either physically or mentally, because the knowledge he has is so highly technical it is like a silken thread which must not be broken. Which of us could solve even a simple mathematical problem if beaten up, frightened, cold, hungry, isolated in squalor or whatever these so-called treatments involve?"

"Drugs," said Gudgeon. "Truth drugs."

Moller shook his head. "You may get a man to mutter a military secret by such means, but the information required from Hopcraft would be enough to fill a big volume with minutiae of methods, details of equipment and, then, the formulae and processing secrets themselves. I doubt if any man alive could produce those co-herently under the influence of drugs. Don't forget Hop-craft has nothing on paper. In his own laboratory, he and his colleagues will have constant access to bench diaries and the like to which they will have needed to refer countless times a day. Data, like timings, temper-atures, volumes . . . all the things a man doesn't need to memorize and which he will always look up just in case his memory should be faulty.

"Hopcraft is faced with reconstructing that informa-tion, gentlemen. Alone, to all intents and purposes—though he may have able scientists alongside him. True, he won't be starting from scratch, because he will know the methods he has himself worked out and adopted. But still a vast undertaking even for a man in tip-top mental and physical condition. And his captors will be aware of one very great obstacle from their point of view. That is that Hopcraft, even if apparently fully co-opera-tive, can fool them by using one wrong word, a complex formula wrong in only one respect, and so on.

"So, everything he gives them will have to be tested at every step. Trials of such a nature, gentlemen, can be lengthy affairs, even assuming Hopcraft has produced correct information throughout. I should also add that, in order to implement certain processes, Rutland's chemical engineers had to design and have built for them certain pieces of apparatus which are not stock items. Even if Hopcraft could remember the details of such constructions, obtaining them would take time."

Moller looked at Masters. "I've run on a bit, George, for obvious reasons."

"Very valuable, none the less, Harry."

"Thank you. I think you will all appreciate why I think our opinion that Hopcraft is still alive is by far the more likely alternative. I would suggest, therefore, that we should proceed on the assumption that he is still extant and confine our activities to pursuing the one end."

"Hear, hear," said Green. "Concentrate on the best bet and don't split our efforts over several possibilities."

Masters was filling his pipe with Warlock Flake. "Any further observations on that? Fred?"

"Now I've heard what Harry had to say, I agree we should assume Hopcraft is still alive."

"Thank you. Major? What about you?"

"I'll go along with Green and Pollock if the Doctor can give us some assurance that the Libyans would have enough nous to leave Hopcraft's treatment to the scientists rather than to the hit-mobs. Prisoners have kicked the bucket before now without spilling the wanted beans because of vicious treatment by jailers."

"A good point. Harry?"

"Of course, I can give no such assurance. But I think this business would have been well thought out before Hopcraft was pinched. The Libyans would have had their scientific team lined up in advance. My belief would be that the scientists would require their musclemen to snatch him and, thereafter, to guard him, but to play no other part. Having said that, I must confess that it is not outside the bounds of possibility that one or two of their scientists are sadistic bastards, as capable of making life uncomfortable for Hopcraft as are the members of a murder squad. But I doubt whether such men would go so far as to kill the toad with the jewel as you have called him. I think, probably, they have been taking a soft line with their man. He has probably had the almost exclusive use of the physical charms of Miss Barcurata, for instance—purely as a stimulant for scientific thought, of course."

"Of course," said Reed.

"Any more observations on that point?" asked Masters. As none was forthcoming he proceeded.

"We assume Hopcraft was abducted from here and that he is still alive. Our job is to find him. The best place from which to start looking is the last place he was known to be. So far we have favoured the sea. Charles, you were to find out whether a small craft could have left the harbour on the night of September the third."

"High water here was at twelve minutes past eleven

that night. A craft such as you are thinking of could have left at any time within an hour each side of that. Probably even longer on the ebb."

"Thank you. Shall we say a bracket of two hours between a quarter past ten and a quarter past twelve."

"That would do it. It was well dark before ten and there was no moon to speak of."

"Good. So all conditions were favourable for spiriting Hopcraft away by sea. We must try to confirm that theory further. Fred, tomorrow, I would like you and Sergeant Reed to go to Bristol. To the port authorities, and discover timings and movements of Libyan ships over that period."

"Fair enough. Specifically, we want to know if one left harbour on that tide?"

"Please. If you are lucky, then I think the coincidence of a Libyan tramp passing down channel a couple of miles from Yourhead that night will strengthen, if not confirm, the sea theory. Bill, Charles and I are going to do some leg work round here."

"With what in mind?" asked Pollock.

"The tent. It stayed put for twenty-four hours, and was then collected. That means that one or more of the people we would like to identify were in this area long enough to correct their mistake. If we could get a line on them . . . well, I'm sure that would be helpful."

"And how," said Green. "We're reverting back to your belief that one of these cottages could have been occupied by the musclemen?"

"It's a possibility. Some of them are let off as holiday cottages. The Major's local knowledge will be useful to us."

"It'll be a pleasure," said Gudgeon, rising to take glasses for refilling.

Masters spoke to Moller. "Something you said a few minutes ago interested me greatly."

"What, particularly, George?"

"The making of special bits of laboratory equipment for the Rutland processes. It occurred to me that Hopcraft's captors may well be after the same sort of thing."

117

"Bound to be, if they've got that far."

"Let us assume that Hopcraft is co-operating with them up to a point—which I hope he is doing for his own sake. In his position I would seize on the provision of those special constructions as a vital delaying tactic."

"I am certain he would do that, too."

"So he will have specified that he needs such things. His captors must try to obtain them, mustn't they?"

"If they wish to succeed, yes."

"Where would Hopcraft—again co-operating up to a point—tell them to go for them?"

Moller grinned. "You're a clever old sod, George. Of course. Hopcraft would say the only people who could supply them are those who hold the specifications for the originals. And he wouldn't hold the specifications for the originals. And he wouldn't hold back at supplying the names, because he'd hope that you would some-how guess that was what he'd do and would, in conse-quence. . . ."

Masters grinned. "Quite right. Send you and Sergeant Berger on a foraging expedition. You will take the Yard Rover, visit Rutland and ask where Hopcraft's chemical engineers had those bits and pieces made up. You will then visit those firms and ask if any of them have been approached for anything like those items. Berger will be with you, with his identity-card to lend weight to your enquiries should it be needed. If even the sniff of a sim-ilar-sized stainless steel nut or bolt has been asked for, I want to know. And the names of the people asking. So dig deep, Harry. And don't let anybody fob you off, either, at the various manufacturers' or at Rutland's."

"I like it," said Green.

"So do I," said Pollock, "and I don't mean that glass of whisky you're holding up to the light. I mean George's idea which sprang from what Harry had to tell us. If ever I needed proof of the value of George's brain-storming sessions, this is it."

"Even if it doesn't come off?"

"Even then. It's the example I'm talking about, Bill.

118

The idea. The chances of it coming off are . . . what? As high as fifty-fifty? But even if they were ten-to-one against it's worth trying."

"A hundred-to-one," growled Green. "You can't afford to miss the slightest whiff of a chance in a game like this. In fact, when one hasn't got to get continuation of evidence, and all the business of means, opportunity and motive, you can play hunches to your heart's content. It's the result that matters, not the usual logical preparation of a case for trial."

Moller was replying to Masters. "This swan you're sending Berger and me on, George, could take time. Several days, in fact. We may have to motor from one end of the country to the other and back again."

"I appreciate that, Harry. The two of you had better take your kit. We'll keep your rooms on at the hotel, of course, but I'd like the job completed before you return. If you have to stay away, please report each evening, by phone, at seven. I'll make a point of always being in my room then. Guarded language, of course."

Berger said: "The strong box, Chief. I'm supposed to be custodian."

"Hand over to Reed, tonight. I'd like this put in it." Masters handed over the letter Moller had brought earlier in the day.

"Time tomorrow morning?" Gudgeon asked Masters.

"Not one of your six o'clock starts, Chas." said Green. "How about nine, George?"

"That should be all right. I don't think we shall need a car, but if we do, I take it there is a garage where I can hire one for the day?"

"Two," said Gudgeon. "They both know me."

"Excellent. I'd rather you hired one. Less likely to cause comment."

"George," said Pollock.

"Yes, Fred?"

"Landing grounds. Are you going to try them?"

"Not yet, not unless we have to. There are none nearby. The ground isn't level enough."

"So I needn't stop off at any aeroclubs?"

"Not tomorrow. If we fail and have to think again, then the need may arise."

"Right."

Masters raised his voice. "Gentlemen, the meeting is over—the official bit, at any rate. Thank you for your help and participation."

"You're not all pushing off, I hope?" said Gudgeon. "It's only just gone half past ten. . . ."

"Berger and I are setting out after having the earliest breakfast we can get," said Moller. "We've got a long day ahead of us."

Green said: "Me, too. You may be sprightly and fit, Chas, but the prospect of twelve hours on the hoof tomorrow is making me feel tired already. Thanks for the party. And arrange to join us for dinner tomorrow. No sloping off beforehand."

"Thanks. I'll make my arrangements accordin', as they say."

Green grinned at him. "You're learning, Chas. Always remember what the lads say. 'Nil desperandum carborundum.'"

"What the hell does that mean?" demanded Berger.

"Latin for 'don't let the bastards grind you down', lad."

Berger raised his eyebrows, but made no reply.

"Thank you, Charles," said Masters. "I've enjoyed being here. Your room, your fire . . . and your company. I'll see you tomorrow."

Masters let Moller, flanked by Reed and Berger, go on ahead as they crossed the road to the esplanade walk. He held Pollock and Green back a while before following.

"You both know there was one possible avenue of exploration I didn't mention in the Major's presence."

"The characters who could have picked up Hopcraft?" asked Pollock.

"That's it. What Bill had to say about following every whiff of a hint must apply here, too. As you know, we have a whiff of a hint about Sid Farries, or at least his boss, Crease. Nothing solid. Just a report of a meeting between Crease and the Cyrenaican Bank employee. But I can't ignore it."

"Have you tried to get any more on them, George?"

"Yes. No luck. So it is the slimmest of hints, except that Crease is a fixer of dirty jobs. He could have arranged the abduction and provided the musclemen."

"Likely," said Green. "You can't hope to have a gang of Libyan toughs operating in a place like Yourhead these days without arousing interest, if not suspicion. It's not what you'd call a cosmopolitan, multi-racial town, is it? For dirty work here, you'd need British villains."

"That's obvious," agreed Pollock. "But I don't know Crease and Farries. Can we get at them?"

"Legally, no," said Masters. "Not at the present stage of the game. But, as Bill said, I'm not after continuation of evidence, I'm after results. So, gents, ideas on what to do about them, please."

"Move in on them," said Green.

"Get in and cut them out," said Pollock.

"Then what?"

"Make them talk," said Pollock.

"How? Where? I can't take them to a nick and apply judge's rules. That would get me nowhere."

"Get Farries," said Green. "Like Fred said, cut him out. He'll cave in as soon as you start talking tough. Where to take him is a different matter. He could start squawking when threatened."

"I've got an idea," said Pollock. "I'll take him. He knows you two are cops from the Yard. But he doesn't know me or where I'm from. I could be just another villain as far as he knows."

"A nice idea," admitted Masters, "but you'd need help, and I don't want to implicate more people than I can help."

"Charley boy," said Green.

"Farries knows him."

"Not when he's all blacked up or got a balaclava on. He'll make Farries talk if anybody will."

"That's what I'm afraid of. He'd kill him. And I'm

121

being serious. I can't take the risk of exposing Farries to Gudgeon, that's why this conversation is not taking place in his hearing."

"Can we think about this a bit more, George?" asked Pollock. "It's not our usual line of country, so we're a bit at a loss. But I'm sure we can find some isolated place to interrogate him. It's just the picking up that'll be the problem. After that . . . well, I can ask a few questions, and with you and your boys present but out of sight, there shouldn't be any trouble."

"Think about it as much as you like," replied Masters. "But we may need an answer fairly soon."

They continued in silence as far as the hotel. "A nightcap in my room, gentlemen?" asked Masters.

"Laid on," said Green. "At least they knew we'd be asking for booze about now. A few cans of ale left out for us."

"Excellent. Just for the three of us, please, Bill. Will you do the necessary?"

"Be with you in two twos, gents."

They sat round the table of the sitting-room in Masters' suite. For a moment or two they busied themselves with their drinks, then Green asked: "You've got something you want to say, George?"

Masters nodded. "I've been having second thoughts about picking up Farries."

"It was obvious you didn't like the idea."

"I don't think any of us did, but it's the sort of operation we must be prepared to indulge in."

"Even though you've as good as said you don't think it necessary?" asked Pollock.

"My second thoughts concerned Farries. If we were to pick him up and he told us everything he knew, what do you think it would amount to?"

"Not much," agreed Green. "But there could be a hint. . . ."

"Of course. But on what reasoning would we be picking him up? Because he would be easy meat?"

"That was the general idea."

"I'm beginning to see what you're driving at, George," said Pollock. "Farries is known to be working for the fixer, Crease. Crease was seen in confab with a Cyrenaican Bank clerk. The Cyrenaican Bank clerk is a contact of Barcurata's—we believe."

"Go on, Fred."

"Farries is only the oily rag out of that lot."

"Quite. If we're right, Crease and Farries were the hired help. All they will know is what they've learned from listening at keyholes."

Green set his tankard down. "You're proposing to go for the bank cashier, is that it?"

"Eissa Al Barcurata isn't here for me to pick up for questioning."

"You're flying high, George."

"In what way?"

"A foreign national, probably an accredited one. Farries is just an old lag, so he wouldn't matter so much, but an alien. . . ?"

"I'd just as soon whoever I picked up was a foreigner as a member of the British public. Far rather, if I believe the foreigner can help me more. But shoot me down if you think you should."

"Shoot you down?" asked Pollock quietly. "What's the difference between the two, particularly if the pick-up is to be in secret? I agree, George. Let's go for the one who can tell us most. After all, what is there to worry about? Your masters gave you virtually a free hand to work outside the law if needs be, didn't they?"

"They certainly said the ends would justify the means, but I interpreted that as implying that the means should be, shall we say, humane?"

"So you don't mind picking this bloke up, but you stop short of pulling his fingernails out, is that it?"

"More or less. I know we would all like to avoid extremes of violence."

"You can take that as read," said Green. "I'm not as young as I was, so even a punch-up would be too violent

123

for me. So where are we? Tomorrow we all try to make stone-bonker sure that Hopcraft was shanghaied from here. All except Moller and Berger, that is, and they'll try to see whether anybody has started to move on the production side. Having got that sewn up, we grab the banker to get further information out of him and decide how we set about getting Hopcraft back. Right?"

"Right. Then, if he's where we think he is, we've got to decide whether we can extricate him in some way or whether, with the proof of his whereabouts that we can hand to them, the government can demand his release."

"Would that work?" asked Pollock sceptically. "I can't see the Libyans agreeing to something like that."

"Blackmail," said Green. "We'd threaten to freeze their funds or put salt down their oil wells." He looked at Masters. "I know, George. No need to look so ferocious about it."

"About what, in particular?" demanded Pollock.

"The final solution," said Green. "A Nazi term, but applicable here."

"What are you talking about now?"

"Don't you see, Fred, that whatever happens, the government is not going to let Libya keep Hopcraft."

Pollock's jaw dropped. "You mean if we fail and diplomatic measures fail, then . . . then some hit-man will be sent out to dispose of him?"

"More or less. Some clandestine operation which will result in a mysterious explosion and fire at the laboratory where he is working. I fancy that is the most likely, to get rid of anything the Libyans may have. They won't be able to complain we've killed him if they've already denied having him."

"God bless my soul," said Pollock. "I can see the dreadful logic of it now, but I must confess that particular conclusion had never occurred to me."

"It's been living with me," said Masters simply. "That's why I'm prepared to break the habit of a lifetime and pick up that bloody bank cashier."

"I'll have another drink, if there is one," said Pollock

weakly. As Green emptied the remnants of the last tin into his glass, he added: "That final solution gets up my nose, George, so get your thinking cap on and see if we can't bring this off some other way."

Masters replied: "Fred, there are other possibilities. We can't waste time, but we've got to do a crumbling action. Each new hint we glean will, I hope, steer us the right way. But I'm not clairvoyant. I can't foresee events—though, as I said, I am sure there are other possibilities. What they are, exactly, depends on what we discover tomorrow or the day after or the day after that. I suggest we get to bed now. It's been a long old day."

5

Gudgeon was waiting with his wind-cheater on when Masters and Green arrived at his cottage the next morning.

"Plan of attack, please," he demanded as he invited them in.

"Can we sit down for a moment?"

"Of course. By the way, my daily, Mrs Shaw, is in the kitchen, so if you don't want her to overhear, keep your voices low. I've told her you are two chaps I met at the pub last night and you're hoping to take a holiday cottage along here later in the year. I got the names of the agents for two or three of them. The others are private people. I've got some of those, too. Mostly they live quite close by."

"Excellent," said Masters. "We know the time of year, so it's a question of asking about lettings at the end of August and the beginning of September."

"You'd like me to do that alone?"

"Do you know any of the people involved?"

"Those who are my neighbours in this row. At least to say good-day to."

"So they wouldn't suspect any police involvement in your enquiries?"

Gudgeon shook his head. "They'll take what I say at its face value."

"And you think you can question them casually to get the information?"

"I'm not untutored in the art of interrogation, you know. I may not be in your league, and some of the tricks

126

I've been taught maybe shouldn't be used among friends and neighbors, but I'll play it gently."

"I'm sure you will. Now, do you happen to know who owns the kiosk and the shops at the near end of the quay?"

"Sorry. They're closed at this time of year and though I'd recognize the assistants. . . ."

"Not to worry. I'll discover who they are."

"Could I suggest you talk to old Barter. He's an old boy employed by the local council to look after the deck-chairs on the quay. They are put away for the winter, of course, but Barter stacks them every night in summer, just behind the kiosk, on the seaward side. He actually ties a tarpaulin over them to keep them dry and to stop any high wind from blowing them away."

"He's likely to be a good informant?"

"That I can't say, but he's there till all hours. The old boy goes to the pub in the evening, at which time a lot of his chairs are still occupied. So he makes his last round after closing time. Your bracket of an hour each side of midnight could actually cover his pottering about."

"What time does the pub close?" asked Green.

"Half past ten."

"Give him ten minutes to down his last few mouthfuls, two or three to say a garrulous goodnight to his cronies. . . ."

"The quay is all of three hundred yards long and Barter doesn't move very fast, particularly if he's folding down and collecting the odd chair."

"Six hundred yards to walk . . ." said Green. "He'd certainly not be through by eleven."

"And old boys like Barter notice anything out of the ordinary," said Gudgeon.

"I'll see Barter," promised Masters. He turned to Green. "I'm leaving the pub to you, Bill. Play it any way you like. Somebody could have noticed, and mentioned, something odd going on that night."

Green nodded his acceptance of the chore.

"I've no idea how long all this is going to take us," said Masters, "but I shall make a point of being at the hotel at one o'clock for half an hour at least, and again at five. We can leave messages for each other, or meet at those times, whichever is most convenient. Actually, Major, I hope you will find time to get there at one for a glass and a sandwich on the firm."

"Thank you. I'll do my best. I'm not one to refuse a drink on the police."

As they left the cottage, Gudgeon had one more question. "By the way, do you happen to know the names of the chaps who could have taken the cottage? I think it would be easier if I had a name to produce."

Masters considered this for a moment. Green shrugged his shoulders as if to indicate that this might be a difficult moment and he wanted none of it.

"We obviously don't know who the villains are," said Masters. "We have just one little hint that a fixer called Crease could be involved, but I very much doubt whether he would appear in person."

"Crease?"

"Call the other Parry," suggested Green. "It sort of rolls off the tongue—Crease and Parry. Come to think of it, it sounds a bit like a firm of house agents. We can all three use the same pair—if we have to mention them, that is."

Masters looked at Green for a moment and then nodded his agreement. Green said, "So long, gents. If I go round the back of the pub, I should get the landlord before he opens."

"I'm just going a few doors along to start with," said Gudgeon.

"And I," said Masters, "will visit the council offices."

"Names of stall holders?" asked Green.

"These things, I believe, come up for renting each year. Do you think I could present myself as a potential kiosk renter or shopkeeper?"

"Not in those trousers. You look as much like a seaside stall holder as Chas looks like a hippy."

"Solicitor acting on behalf of clients?"

"More like it. But don't get in too deep."

The publican was about Green's age. The licence over the door had given his name as Stanley Edward Grace. Green, going round to the back of the building had found him there, wearing woollen cap and muffler, and using a modern electric chain-saw to cut logs from odd lengths of timber, presumably from the same source as those used by Gudgeon.

Green caught his attention by moving round the saw-horse till he stood full in the man's view. As soon as the log fell, the publican took his finger off the switch and pumped a couple of squirts of oil on to the chain while he waited for Green to speak.

"Are you the landlord?"

"That's me. What can I do for you?"

"Answer a few questions, I hope."

Grace looked warily at Green. "Why?"

"Because I'd like to know the answers, chum."

"And who are you?"

"Certainly not somebody who's come to cause you any trouble, mate. I'm not interested in how you run your house. I'm from the Home Office, actually."

"Not a cop?"

"More of a civil servant."

"And what do the civil service want with me?"

"With you, personally? Nothing. We're trying to trace a chap who disappeared."

"What would I know about somebody who disappeared? Anyhow, when was it?"

"The end of last summer actually."

"And you expect me to be able to help?"

"All I'm asking is that you let me tell you the circumstances, then we'll see if you can help. Maybe you can't, but I've got to try everything I can to find him. My name's Bill Green, by the way."

"Mine's Stan Grace. Now, what's it all about?"

"It concerns a tent that was pitched on the Lawn one day and left empty. . . ."

"Wait a minute! I did hear something about that now you come to mention it."

"There you are then, Stan. D'you think we could just go inside for a little talk? This wind's not all that hot."

Stan led the way into the still-curtained public bar. As he went along the passage leading to it, he shouted through a door: "Mother!"

"She's upstairs making the beds," replied a younger woman's voice.

"Tell her I'm in the public with an official caller and the bread's not come yet. Ask her to get on to them about it."

"Right, Stan."

Grace opened the curtains and invited Green to take a seat at a small table neatly laid out with a clean ashtray and four beer-mats.

"Now then! Let's hear all about it. I haven't got all day you know."

"As far as we can make out, this chap—his name's Arthur—was backpacking and studying birds and flowers along the way. We reckon he came down that little hill footpath after dark one night last summer and found himself on that big, flat grass patch of yours. He must have thought that was a good place to pitch his tent. . . ."

"Which isn't allowed," said Stan. "There's a notice the size of that wall saying so."

"That's right. But it faces outwards, this way. That's why we think he came from the other end and didn't see the notice. Anyhow, he put his tent up. The next day there was nothing to be seen of him."

"Drownded, more than likely," said Grace.

"You reckon he went swimming in the dark?"

"Sounds like it."

"Then who pinched his belongings the next night? The cops didn't."

"Well, anybody could have done that. Yobs, for instance."

"Right. And that's where you come in."

"Me? Why?"

"Most yobs like a drink. I wondered if they'd come in here. . . ."

"I watch it."

"You don't get many kids in here then?"

"Some, in the summer. But we get older chaps mostly. Well, not all old, because we get the lifeboat crew and chaps from the gasworks besides our regulars from round about. And in the summer we get people off the yachts and cruisers that put in. Lunchtimes we get the ordinary family men. Visitors, you know. The kiosk sells lemonade and buns for the kids. The men come in for a pint and a ploughman's. There's a lot of people sit out on the quay, you know. That wall on the seaward side makes a sun trap and I've known as many as two hundred and fifty deck-chairs occupied along there. But they're family men, the sort that sit there. They'd not put up with yobs. Besides, we're too far out for the nasties. There's more for them in the town proper—amusement arcades with pin-tables and juke-boxes. That sort of thing."

"I get the picture," said Green, offering his cigarette packet. "So if any lads who might fancy pinching a camper's tent did come in, the occasion would stick out like the feather in my missus' best hat."

"Unless they were quiet, it would."

"Any thoughts about it?"

"We had a broken window, last summer, I remember. When would it be, now? June, July perhaps."

"I'm talking about September the third. That was the night—"

Green was interrupted. "Stan," called a woman's voice. "Stan, are you going to open up today? Or can we all go off?"

"My old woman," said Stan apologetically. "Look, I've got one or two things to do. . . ."

"I'll sit here," said Green. "When you've got a few minutes perhaps we could carry on."

131

"Yeah. I've thought of something." Stan got to his feet. "In about five minutes then. I'll be back behind the bar."

"Good," replied Green. "I'll be able to have one for the good of the house."

"We have five-year agreements," said the female clerk in the Treasurer's Office. "And this isn't the year for them to come up for renewal."

"Do you allow the tenants to sub-let?" Masters asked.

"It's against the council rules."

"But if for any reason they should wish to relinquish their tenancies before the five years are up, what then? Five years is a long time and anything could happen to cause tenants to want to pull out."

"It doesn't happen. The people who run the kiosk and shops have all done it for years. Their families follow on, usually, if there's a death or ill-health."

"I see. My client was born here. Frankly I have advised him not to entertain the idea of coming back to take a property. . . ."

"Why not, pray?"

"Because what he has in mind would be for the summer months only. I told him to come back to Yourhead by all means, but to take a property from which he could trade the whole year round."

"Oh, I see. Well, of course, the other shop premises in the town don't belong to the council. It's only those on the esplanade and the quay that are our property."

"Quite. Thank you very much for your help. I'll give my client your views, but he is so set on having one of your properties that he is certain to ask if I have approached the current tenants to see if one of them is prepared to relinquish in his favour."

"They won't, as I told you."

"Quite. I know I won't succeed. Indeed I hope I don't. But I wonder if you would mind giving me their names and addresses so that I could just have a quick word with them—so as to be able to assure my client I have made every effort. . ."

"Not allowed. We can't disclose names and addresses."

"That's what I feared. I shall have to go to the landlord of the public house at the end of the quay. He won't be bound by the same restrictions. . . ."

"I'll let you have them. But don't say where you got them from."

"I am obliged to you." He waited for a few moments while she wrote, left-handed, the list of names and addresses. As she handed it to him, he asked: "Would you allow me to repay kindness with kindness? Can you leave your office to take a cup of coffee with me? I see there's a pastry-cook's shop, not far away with a café above it. Would you care to join me?"

Evidently the pressure of work in the council offices of a small seaside resort in the winter months was not so great as to put an unscheduled coffee break out of the question. Inside five minutes, Masters found himself sitting over coffee and doughnuts with Miss Mary Jewell. He found it tedious, chiefly because he begrudged the time, but also because he found he was having to parry questions from the inquisitive Miss Jewell as to the identity of his mysterious client and the leasing of shops and properties elsewhere in the country. At length, his companion glanced at her watch and jumped to her feet. "Goodness, look at the time. I said I'd only be gone a few minutes. They'll be wondering where I am."

Thankfully, Masters escorted her back to the council offices.

"Are you staying in Yourhead, Mr Masters?"

"I put up at the Water's Edge Hotel."

"How long are you staying?"

"For a day or two longer, perhaps. I can't really say, but I have a little more business round here and now I have arrived and find it so pleasant, I may even take a short holiday."

"Won't your wife mind about that?"

Understanding the purpose of the question. Masters replied: "The relationship between my wife and me is such that . . . well, I honestly don't think she will expect me to rush back."

He saw that his answer had the effect he had expected. Miss Jewell said, "In that case perhaps we shall meet again."

"If we do, it will be my pleasure," said Masters. "Goodbye, Miss Jewell. Thank you for your help and for your delightful company."

"Thank you, Mr Masters."

It was no great difficulty to locate the addresses he had been given. At strategic points in the town were large street maps of the "You are here" variety. A few minutes spent consulting one of them enabled him to work out the most economic route to take to embrace all the addresses.

It was while he was walking towards the first of them that he remembered Barter, the deck-chair attendant. He had obviously not been able to ask Miss Jewell for this information. He made a mental note to ask the shop-keepers he hoped he was about to see.

Gudgeon rapped on the door of a woman who lived several doors away from him.

"Good morning, Mrs Hillstead."

"Good morning, Major. You're out and about bright and early for a coldish day. I suppose it was those two visitors calling on you so early that got you away from the fireside?"

"Something like that, Mrs Hillstead."

"Come in then, Major. We don't want to stand out here all day. I'm just in the middle of doing the veggies for Cornish pasties. Eddie likes them on days like this. He likes them turned over, you know, and as big as a dinner plate. Not those little things nipped together on top. He says those are all skirt and no dinner."

"Sorry to interrupt you at your chores, but my friends asked me to get the rates you charge for summer letting of your other cottage."

"Depends, dear."

"What on?"

"Time of season, how many there'll be of them. I mean two men like that wouldn't come on holiday alone, would they?"

"Hardly. They've both got wives."

"So there'd be four. When would they want to come?"

"Do you know, Mrs Hillstead, I didn't think to ask them."

"Well, you'll have to get the dates." With a carrot in one hand and a knife in the other, she peered at a year-planning calendar pinned to the kitchen wall. "It's gone, you see, the last two weeks in May, all June, and the last fortnight in August. There's a tentative for the middle fortnight of July, though I don't like that because it cuts across two letting periods if you see what I mean. Another tentative for the first half of August, so you see all that's really left is probably a fortnight in July, and after that I'm afraid it's September."

Gudgeon made a careful note of the dates. They were going to be his let-out for not confirming the booking.

"I'll tell them," he promised. As he was turning away, he stopped and turned back, "Oh, by the way, Mrs Hillstead, I've been meaning to ask you this for months."

"What, Major?"

"Last year—the first week in September, actually. I remember the date because it's the one and only time that Ernie's ever come up for me and I got a few bob out of it. At that time I caught sight of two chaps who I thought I knew years back. I couldn't go out after them because I had somebody in the house with me, but my guest at the time said he thought they were staying in a cottage along here. If they were the men I thought they were—two of my former sergeants, their names were Crease and Parry. Do they ring any bells with you, Mrs Hillstead?"

She shook her head as she put her knife down and wiped her hands on her apron. "I'm sure they don't, but I'll look in my book for you." From among a small heap of cookery books on a pine shelf, she took a ledger. "Beginning of September, you said," as she turned the pages. "Sorry, Major, the Netherfield family had it then—father, mother and two small children."

"Thank you, Mrs Hillstead. I'll let my friends know your vacant dates and they can get in touch with you themselves if they want to know anything else."

"That's right, Major. . . . Oh! and if you want to know about your two sergeants, why don't you slip along and ask Beryl Lawson. She's got two lets, right at the end. They stand back a bit, with a sort of open garage under one of the bedrooms. But there, you know them as well as I do."

"Unfortunately I don't know Mrs Lawson except to say good morning to."

"Get away with you. She'd love you to call. She's a youngish widow with a bit of property and you're a well-set-up widower in your prime. She'd be daft if she didn't want to see you."

Gudgeon laughed. "If she's as big a matchmaker as you appear to be, Mrs Hillstead, I'd better steer clear."

"She's nice looking. A man like you needs a bit of female company occasionally."

"Does it show that much?"

"Get on with you, Major, I want to finish these pasties."

Gudgeon saw himself out. When it came to women, he was basically a shy man, and he had not relished the prospect of visiting Beryl Lawson whom, as he had said to Mrs Hillstead, he did not know except by sight. After what Mrs Hillstead had said, he felt even more disinclined to pay the visit, but a strong sense of duty took him, nevertheless, to the front door of Mrs Lawson's cottage.

Far from being a predatory female, Beryl Lawson proved to be a delightful, personable woman. She invited Gudgeon in and offered him some of the coffee she was preparing. "I'm having my elevenses a bit early, because I'm on duty at the library after lunch. So I have to have a snack soon after twelve."

Much to his surprise, Gudgeon found himself making

a mental note to use the public library more often. But aloud, he used the same story, in the same sequence as with Mrs Hillstead.

"The first week in September, Major? Crease and Parry? No, I don't think so, but I have last year's bookings handy. I have to keep them for making up the dreaded income tax form . . . let me see. No, not in either cottage. The Armour family was in number sixty and . . ." She turned the page. "Oh, yes, I remember. Mr Juri, a foreign gentleman had it—with another man."

"A foreigner? Do you often let to foreigners?"

"Not often. But only because they are not usual customers."

"Juri. What nationality would he be?"

"I've no idea. Mediterranean of some sort, I think, but terribly westernized. Spoke beautiful English. That's why I was surprised that he should have the companion he did. A real Cockney tough, he seemed to me."

"What was his name?"

"I don't remember exactly. I haven't got it down, because it was Mr Juri who rented the cottage and paid for it. It was a bit of luck for me—and them—really, because I'd had a cancellation and so when they came along asking on the Saturday, and offering to pay in advance, I let them have the cottage."

"Isn't it a bit risky? Letting just like that, I mean?"

"It could be, particularly with just two men alone, but Mr Juri had his fiancée with him . . . Tessa, I think he called her . . . so it seemed as if it would be all right."

"And was it?"

"Perfectly. Actually, they went home a day early, but they left the cottage very clean and tidy and they brought the key back."

"So," said Gudgeon getting to his feet, "you didn't have my two former colleagues, Crease and Parry. . . ."

Mrs Lawson put her hand to her mouth. "Parry! Parry! No, his name wasn't Parry."

"Whose name?"

"The Cockney man's. Not Parry, but something like

137

that. Parish, would it be? Parry, Parish . . . well something like that with an 'a' vowel sound in it."

"Not to worry, Mrs Lawson," replied Gudgeon, conscious of a feeling of elation at having ferreted out a Mediterranean gentleman, a cockney tough and a girl called Tessa—or was it Essa? He guessed his part was over. The thing now was to report to Masters.

Green waited patiently in the bar, which was redolent of bitter beer, spray polish and smoke. He could hear various noises from other parts of the house and tried to define them, with little luck except for the crossfire of voices. Then Stan returned. He had smartened himself up somewhat, chiefly by taking off cap, muffler and anorak. He crossed straight to the fireplace with a box of matches in his hand.

"I'd best get this going," he said, as he crouched before the grate. "Not that there'll be all that many in for a bit yet, but I've got to be here and it cheers the place up. Besides, it costs little or nothing. We get a deal of wood washed up. It burns well once it's dried."

As the flames began to lick round the kindling of the laid fire, Stan straightened up and moved across to unbolt the door. He slid the fastening back and then moved towards the bar. "It's all go," he said to Green as he passed to open the flap. He passed through, closing the gap behind him. Then he pressed switches and lights came on. Then he shouted through the door for a bowl of washing water. As soon as the young woman had carried that in and departed, he said to Green: "Now, what's it to be?"

"On me," said Green getting to his feet and moving to the bar. "What're you having, Stan?"

"It's a bit early for me."

"And me. But I'm having half of bitter, so break your own rule and join me before you get busy."

Stan pulled the drinks and accepted the money.

"Cheers."

"Cheers," replied Green.

"Now, about this bloke you're looking for," said Stan, putting his tankard down. "Arthur, wannit?"

"That's him. Disappeared on September the third."

"Ah, that's it." Stan leaned forward, elbows on the bar. "I knew you'd said summats which brought something to mind. It was the date. September the third."

"Oh yes?" murmured Green.

"Big night here, always, September the third."

"Why's that?"

"It's the anniversary of the day war broke out in thirty-nine."

Green nodded. "I hadn't forgotten that, but why should it be so important forty or fifty years on?"

"It's a bit of a long story."

"I've got all morning."

"You'll be old enough, I daresay, to remember that militia call-up of lads a few months before war broke out."

Green nodded.

"Then you'll also remember that the arguing about it went on for months and months before it happened, because there'd never been conscription in peacetime in this country before. There were a lot of people against it, including members of the government who, besides not wanting it, felt the country couldn't afford it, which is a bit of a laugh seeing what came later on in the year."

"I remember all that," said Green.

"Well, in order to cut the cost, the government cut the categories of those liable to call-up. For instance, it was said that anybody in the TA would be exempt."

"With the result that thousands of youngsters joined the Terriers, I seem to remember."

"Right. Quite a few of us from round here did. There was a Drill Hall in Yourhead at that time, with a couple of dozen chaps doing drills under a sergeant and a First War Officer. By the time we'd signed on round here we'd got a half-company of Service Corps. Chaps had come in from farms and villages round about as well as from

Yourhead itself. My old dad had this house then, and there were eight or nine of us drinkers from this pub alone who joined up.

"Then, as you probably know, two or three days before war was declared we were mobilized. What a lark that was. We reported to the drill hall and a trickle of mob kit started coming through. We slept on the floor of the hall and in two or three of the old bell tents we had there and which were put up on the patch of ground outside. Fortunately, it was good weather.

"But after the first couple of days we were just left hanging about. Bits of drill here and there and the odd bit of kit being issued, but nothing to keep a mob of active young men really busy. And then came Sunday. Of course, we were still weekend minded in those early days, so they let everybody who wasn't on stag duty go off for the day. Then war was declared at eleven o'clock. The pub wasn't open by then—half eleven on Sundays in those days. So it was that night that me and my mates found ourselves all together in here, in uniform and wanting to have a few quick beers before reporting back for lights-out at ten fifteen.

"As I said, there were eight or nine of us. Nine actually. We got a few beers on board, and then we started talking as anybody would on the day a big war was declared. Who'd still be alive by the time it was finished and so on. Quite maudlin we got, because a lot of civvies were buying us lads in uniform a fair amount of beer.

"Anyhow, the upshot was that we swore a solemn oath between us that after it was all over, the survivors, if there were any, would meet in this bar on the night of September the third, every year. And that's what we done, true to our word. Eight of us got back, actually. Surprising, isn't it?"

"In a way," agreed Green. "Still, one in nine dead is over eleven per cent and you weren't infantry or tanks or sappers lifting mines. What I mean is, you didn't spend all your time up front. You just paid visits like."

"That's right. I hadn't looked at it that way before.

Anyhow, eight of us got back and a couple have died since, so there's still six of us, all in our middle sixties, and we make a point of being here on the right day."

"Not as noisy these days though, is it?"

"No. But you'd be surprised. Towards closing time we get all the old songs. You know—'Our Sergeant Major is one of the Forty Thieves and the Q Bloke's the other Thirty-Nine.' Remember that one?"

Green nodded and then said, "So you were all here on the night of September the third."

"That's right. And that's when the ambulance appeared."

"Ambulance?" queried Green, with a faint sensation of having struck oil. "What happened? Did somebody get clobbered?"

"Nothing like that, actually. It wasn't a real ambulance."

"No?"

"P'raps you won't remember if you weren't in the Service Corps. . . ."

"I wasn't."

"Oh, well then, you won't remember the Dodge vans we sometimes got from America."

"We called them Bread Vans," said Green. "Ours were painted white when they came and they were just like bakers' delivery wagons. We used them as office trucks."

"That's them," said Stan, "only we called them Bed Pans because we used them as ambulances for walking wounded. And it was a van just like that that came here that night."

"To the pub?"

"Not to the pub actually. If you look out of that right-hand window over there. . . ." He got up and led the way. ". . . you'll see a little car-park cut out of the hillside." He stopped and pointed. "See it? That building is the public loo. Gents this end, ladies the other. The van pulled up alongside."

They turned away from the window. "Some of our mob saw it and the likeness to the old Bed Pans struck them

141

immediately. There was a bit of joshing about somebody being thoughtful enough to send a blood wagon to take them home because they were Harry Flatters and couldn't drive themselves. But there was something funny about that van."

"In what way?"

"First off, it parked in the spot right alongside the gents, when it had got the whole of the car-park to chose from, and nobody does that from choice. I'm not saying the loos aren't clean, they are, but after a long hot day with plenty of use they begin to niffle a bit. It wouldn't have been so bad if the driver hadn't stayed in it. One of the lads said that the bloke had parked so close he must have been bursting for a pee and didn't reckon he could make the distance across the park. That sounded fair enough, but the driver didn't move. Nobody got out of that Bed Pan at all."

"So what happened?"

"The lads were all set to go and take it over. For a lark, like. I had to try and stop 'em, because I didn't want my place getting a bad name with the police. Two of them actually went outside, and I was just going to go after them when they came back. They said they'd been beaten to it. There'd been a bit of a scuffle round the van and they were sensible enough to steer clear of that. That's all there was to it, but I noticed when a couple of taxis came to take the lads away and I went outside to see them off, that the Bed Pan had gone."

"Had you ever seen it before?"

"No, or I'd have noticed it. Nor since."

"Can you say what the bloke in the cab looked like?"

"You can't, can you, through a windscreen? And he never dismounted, as I've told you, unless he did when there was the scuffle."

"And nothing more happened that night that was out of the ordinary?"

"No. Everything was just normal. Mark you, we

weren't looking for chaps going missing. We were enjoying our reunion."

"Of course. Thanks, Stan. Now, let's have another one, then I'll have to push off."

Masters was having no luck. He tramped round Yourhead to four different addresses. All the shop and kiosk owners remembered the day when the empty tent had been left on the Lawn, but nothing more. They closed their premises at half past seven at night and then hurried home for food and rest after a long day on their feet.

He located Barter, the deck-chair attendant. He had seen nothing, nor had he noticed any strange launch that had slipped out of the little harbour overnight. "And I'd know," he had said. "I keep my eye on them. I've known one or two take my chairs down so they can sit on their decks in comfort at our expense, drinking gin an' tonic. I watch it. If I didn't, I would lose some chairs."

And with that, Masters had to be content. It was almost ten to one as he turned down the High Street to make his way to the Water's Edge Hotel. When he arrived, he found Green and Gudgeon waiting for him.

"You look as deflated as Santa Claus on Boxing Day," said Green. "I'll whistle you up a drink while you take your coat up. Make it snappy."

When Masters returned, Green said: "I know there's no talking allowed down here, but can I take it you've not had a good morning?"

Masters sipped his beer. "Ghastly, actually. I found myself having to entertain a local government official, to coffee. A Miss Jewell. She wanted to know if I was married."

"And being the perfect gent, you admitted to having a wife."

Masters nodded. "But I'm afraid I gave the impression that we are often parted."

"Which is true," grunted Green, "but you meant it in another way. To keep the door open?"

"Yes. I felt I might need her help again."

Green grinned. "Don't worry. I won't tell Wanda. What's this Miss Jewell like?"

"Difficult to describe," replied Masters, "but from the way she questioned me about my movements it wouldn't surprise me if you were to get a chance to see her for yourself. I have a suspicion she may bowl in here for drinks or dinner in the next few days."

Green laughed. "I can't wait. Be a sport, George. Give her a ring and invite her along."

Masters didn't reply. Green, seeing a young waiter poke his head round the door, beckoned him and ordered sandwiches for three.

"We'll talk in one of the shelters," said Masters after lunch. "The nearest one to here if it is unoccupied, so that we can see if any of the others get back to the hotel. It shouldn't be too windy on the landward side."

They were in luck. Nobody else seemed to want to sit in the open air. One or two people walked dogs along the esplanade, and the odd car, sticking to the restricted speed limit, passed gently along the road towards the harbour, most of them returning a few minutes later.

Masters had his say first. When he got to the end, Green said: "You sucked a dry one there, George."

"The shopkeepers don't worry me. I didn't expect anything of them. But old Barter . . . well, he's a shrewd old sinner, with eyes like a hawk. He was at the pub that night, and he did go along the quay and he neither saw nor heard anything untoward. The same with craft in the harbour. He said none had left on that night's tide, because if they had done, they couldn't have got back to their moorings by the time he was back on duty next morning. Of course, he could have made a mistake, and one might have taken off, which he doesn't remember. But that's no good to us. We want proof, and with his denial. . . ."

"Forget that for a moment, George. Don't take it in isolation. I don't know what Chas has got to report, be-

144

cause we didn't talk in the hotel, but I think I have something which could just prove to be of use."

"I'm glad to hear it, Bill. I'd begun to think all my theorizing had been faulty, but if you have something. . . ."

"So have I," said Gudgeon. "And I'd say what I learnt suggests that your theory is right, at least in part."

"Better and better," said Masters. "I'm all ears, gentlemen. Who's going to begin?"

"Guests first," said Green. "Fire away, Chas."

Gudgeon gave a very succinct report.

"Juri and Tessa and Parry or Parish," said Masters quietly. "Well done, Charles."

"It must be as you envisaged, George," said Gudgeon, using Masters' christian name for the first time. "Tessa must be Essa Bari. Mrs Lawson got it wrong, misheard it or something. Easy enough to do with uncommon names. Then Juri, a Mediterranean gentleman, Mrs Lawson called him. Well, I know that could be Spanish, French, Italian, Greek or what have you, but it could also be Libyan. At least, I reckon so, because everybody would call an Italian an Italian and a Greek a Greek if they were obviously so."

"Quite right, Chas," said Green.

Gudgeon turned to him. "And there's your suggestion of a name for the other man. Parry! If that was a guess or just a name off the top of your head, it was a damn close thing."

"Not exactly a guess, Chas."

"I thought not."

"You see, we've heard that there's a strong-arm bloke working for this fixer, Crease, you've heard George mention, who uses a name like that. We've no evidence against him, of course, or we'd have run him in. And we've no proof he's mixed up in this business, but as we wanted a name, and the possibility that this Parry or Parish is implicated, I thought I'd just mention it to you as a sort of cockshy."

"It seems as if you could have bagged a coconut then, doesn't it?"

"It sometimes happens like that," murmured Green. "You've got to learn to take the smooth with the rough in this game."

"So I'm learning. But nobody thought to mention this chap Parry to me."

"Because had we done so," said Masters, "it could have misled you. Just to drop it in like Bill did was fairly reasonable, because we had no proof he was implicated. And please don't forget I did tell you on my first visit to your cottage that I thought a number of villains might have tramped past your front door. At that time I said they could be people who might recognize you or you them. I had to put it that way, because we had no names, nor did I know who might be known to you or vice versa. It is quite tricky working in the dark, Charles. There's no clearly defined enemy front line to fire at."

"I understand that, George. Sorry if I sounded too offended. I'm well aware that you've trusted me a hell of a lot with secrets I've no right to know."

"Good. Now, we'd better hear what Bill can tell us."

Green's recall was so very good that his report was a full one and took much longer to tell than had Gudgeon's. The other two heard him out in silence.

"A scuffle?" said Masters when Green had finished. "You've interpreted that, Bill, haven't you?"

"That's when they took Hopcraft," admitted Green. "It sticks out a mile. They knew he'd have to visit the loo. It's the one place everybody does have to visit. So they parked there, right alongside it and took him. No distance to carry or frogmarch him. They waited in that van like spiders waiting for a fly. The girl lured him to Yourhead. To the very spot they wanted. And then, bingo! Nobody saw it but a couple of the old and bold who were half shot at by that time and didn't realize what was happening. It fits, George."

"So it does, Bill. And it destroys all my nice theories."

"How do you make that out?" asked Gudgeon. "You theorized that the kidnappers would take a holiday cottage here, and they did. You theorized they would take him on the car-park and they did. You thought they had taken him across to a small craft in the harbour. It now seems that bit was wrong. But not basically. Instead of using a boat to put him aboard a tramp steamer coming down channel, they used a vehicle to carry him up to Bristol and put him on board there, at the docks."

Masters smiled. "Thanks, Charles, but I know my thinking behind all this has been wrong."

"How come?" demanded Green.

"I surmised that the girl lured Hopcraft to Yourhead. Why? Because that was the best place suited to their abducting him. Why was it best? Because they could take him off in a small boat. And so on. But now we think they picked him up in a vehicle and carried him off to Bristol. But Bristol is sixty miles away. That's a long way to go with a prisoner if you don't have to, particularly as there are numerous places between here and there which would have suited their purpose just as well for kidnapping, and been very much easier and quicker for transporting."

"So you reckon your thinking has been all wrong, just on account of that, do you?"

"Yes. It seems to me that the girl didn't lure him here. I reckon Hopcraft said this was where he was intending to come."

"And they made their plans accordingly. What's wrong with that? It involved a journey of sixty miles to Bristol. So what?"

"Sorry, Bill, but I don't like it. If they'd wanted to cart him out of Bristol, they'd have made use of Barcurata's charms to get him much nearer there. Hopcraft's relationship with that girl was a distinct asset to them, but they didn't use it—at least not to the full. I'm wondering why, and I know the basis of my theories has been shown up as faulty."

"But it led you here," objected Gudgeon.

"An empty tent did. My thinking didn't. There's something wrong, Bill. What is it?"

"Search me, George. I thought we were doing all right.

But you can't make any decisions until you hear from Pollock and Moller. And I'll tell you what. Your theory may be wrong, but at least it's flexible enough to trim to meet facts. Why call it a theory at all? You formed a plan to get things moving. We've got moving. Rejig the plan to take account of the new facts we've unearthed."

Masters took out his brassy tin of Warlock Flake and chose a sliver to rub down for his pipe. He waited a few moments before replying. "I've no option but to wait to hear what Pollock has discovered," he said, "so anything we chew over now could be useless speculation."

"In that case," said Gudgeon, "why not walk along to the cottage and have a cup of tea."

"Good idea, Chas," said Green. "It's four o'clock and all's well as far as I'm concerned." He got to his feet. "Come on, George. The cup that cheers awaits you."

"Come and have dinner tonight, Charles," said Masters as they left the cottage. "Join us in the residents' bar at half past six."

"Right. You'll have to step out if you're going to be in your room for five to take phone calls."

Masters and Green made their way towards the Water's Edge Hotel in the gathering darkness. Green said: "You're a lot more cheerful than you were an hour ago, George. I'll have to tell Chas his brew did the trick."

"Very nice, it was," conceded Masters.

"But?"

"I've had a thought, Bill."

"I might have known it. Changed your theory to take account of changed facts, have you?"

"Not quite. Would you care to hear it, just to see what you think?"

"Try me."

Masters spoke for most of the way back. As they stopped before crossing the road to reach the hotel, Green said: "If you're right, it could make things easier. There'll be a lot of hard work involved, but it will be better from our point of view. So now all we've got to do is hope Fred Pollock failed miserably."

"They're not back yet, Bill. The car isn't here."

At a quarter to six, when Masters, having bathed, was tying his tie, Green tapped at the door.

"They're back, George. I've just seen young Reed. They'll be along here as soon as they've cleaned up and changed."

"Good. Have a pew, Bill, or alternatively, make yourself useful and ask for some booze to be sent up. Personally, I'd like a gin. Ask for a bottle, half a dozen tonics and a saucerful of sliced lemon—if that'll suit you and the others."

"Couldn't be better. Are you sure the budget for Operation Hosepipe can stand it?"

"I was told to spare no expense," replied Masters, putting on his jacket. "And I'm operating with far fewer people than the powers-that-be envisaged."

While he distributed his impedimenta into his pockets, Green used the house phone to order the tray. As he came to the end of the order, the receptionist said: "Would you please hold on. There's a call coming in for Mr Masters."

It was Berger.

"Chief, the doc and I are in Brum. We're staying the night."

"Fine. Does that signify success or failure?"

"Sorry, Chief. Nothing doing our end."

"But Dr Moller has decided to stay over?"

"He asked me to say there may still be what he calls a forlorn hope, Chief, and I'm to tell you he's not too sanguine about it but he's going to try it, just for laughs. That's why we're staying here. I've no idea where we'll be off to tomorrow."

"Please ask him to pursue any ideas he may have and keep him up to it."

"Understood, Chief."

Masters put the phone down.

"No luck from Moller?"

"None. Complete failure so far. I take that to mean on the specialist equipment side. Obviously Berger couldn't say much, but Moller's got something else to try. No hint of what it may be."

"Cheer up, George. It isn't all collapsing around your ears, you know."

Pollock and the waiter arrived at virtually the same moment. Reed was a few moments later.

"Today," said Green, as he poured the drinks, "has not been one of total success. George is feeling in two minds about things, so we're having shorts to make us all feel better."

"And I must say I can do with this," said Pollock. "Young Reed and I have had a trying day."

"Ah!" said Masters.

"What does that exclamation signify?" asked Pollock.

"The answer to your question could appear shortly," replied Masters. "Meanwhile . . . Reed, would you mind ringing reception and asking them to send the Major up here when he arrives. I said we'd be in the residents' bar, but I don't think we will." He turned to Pollock. "Fred, I'm going to ask you to give us your report as soon as you feel sufficiently refreshed, then you can hear what we've managed to do and not do."

"I see. Patchy was it?"

"You could call it that."

"In that case, Sergeant Reed and I aren't going to make your day."

"Shall we go and sit down? Bring the tray, please, Bill."

When they were all seated in the sitting-room of the suite, Pollock said: "There is nothing to report, George. We went to the docks—to several docks, actually—and spoke to the harbour staffs. They all looked up their records for us. A Libyan ship left Bristol on the twelfth of August, which is almost a month before the date we're interested in, and another didn't arrive until the ninth of September."

"That knocks a hole in things," grunted Green.

"It certainly does," went on Pollock. "You know, George, I was so certain you were right I couldn't believe it. So I asked the harbour master's office if it was possible to check whether the ship that left in August could have called in and been delayed at any other British port. They thought not as she'd been cleared for Tripoli, but to make sure I asked to borrow a phone and a list of numbers for every possible port—big ones like Cardiff and Pembroke and all the little ones where a tramp could put in. We spent hours on that bloody phone and drew a blank everywhere. Your lad even called Gibraltar, and we heard she had passed through the straits there on the twenty-first of August." He spread his hands. "No good, George. That idea's a non-starter."

Masters nodded. "I'm sorry about that, Fred."

"No need for you to be sorry, mate. It's all our ideas being shot to ribbons that niggles me."

There was a knock at the bedroom door. Reed got up to answer it, and ushered in the Major.

"Just in time, Charles. Sit down and have a drink. Fred Pollock has just told us that no Libyan ship left Bristol within days of the right time. Now you've arrived, I want you to report on your efforts this morning and, after you, Bill can have his say." He looked across at Pollock. "Like you, Fred, I drew a blank. The only word I got was from the deck-chair attendant who told me that all the small boats that were in the harbour on the evening of the third were still there on the morning of the fourth, which meant they hadn't been out or they wouldn't have got back in again on account of the state of the tide."

"I've been thinking about that," said Gudgeon, "and it's not strictly true. The matter is purely academic now, of course, but if the journeys, both out and in, were of short duration, a speedy craft could easily have done both inside the span of one tide. Even the most sluggish of those cruisers can do seven knots. Well, two miles out and two miles back again, in theory should take such a craft not much more than half an hour. Give them double that, and they could still achieve the two journeys within the span of one tide."

"Are you trying to make a point, Chas?" asked Green. "I mean, if the matter of the shore to ship transfer is academic. . . ."

"I was, actually, making a point," said Gudgeon. "I suggested George should consult Barter, whom I extolled as likely to be an expert witness. Now I'm proving to you that I was wrong and that we'd all do well not to trust experts too much."

"That, Chas," said Green, "is a very good point indeed. I'm very much with the bloke who defined an expert."

"How defined?" asked Gudgeon.

"Ex is an unknown quantity, and a spurt is a little squirt under pressure."

"I like it," said Pollock. "And I'll remember it."

Masters said: "I think we'd better push on, gentlemen. Help yourselves to drinks, please, without waiting to be asked. While we're talking, that is. Meantime, Fred, I'd like you to listen to what both Charles and Bill have to report."

Gudgeon and Green reported in turn, much as they had done earlier in the afternoon.

"So," said Pollock heavily, "what's it all about? To me it looks as if they never intended to take him out by sea. We've arrived at some of the right answers, George, but by the wrong route."

"It's nice of you to say we, Fred, when the whole business was mine, and so the mistake was mine. However, we've got to do our best to salvage something from the wreck. Now, I know everybody has had a hard day, so I'm not proposing that we should get down to serious work again tonight. But lest some of us think there is no apparent way ahead, I'd just like to put a few of my own thoughts to you to chew over individually.

"There are several possibilities to consider. The first is that they intended to take Hopcraft out from Yourhead harbour, just as I had envisaged. What if the ship they had intended to put him on was the one which arrived in Bristol on the ninth? Say that it was due on the first or second of the month but was delayed. Not perhaps at any other port of call, but at Tripoli itself. Engine repairs or just plain incompetence in getting its load to the dockside and on board."

Green growled, "That's more than likely."

"It's a distinct possibility," agreed Pollock.

"If that is a correct assumption," continued Masters, "it means that the kidnappers had hurriedly to lay on an alternative plan, namely to take Hopcraft and transport him elsewhere by vehicle.

"This in turn might suggest that they kept him hidden away somewhere until they could put him on board the delayed ship."

"Feasible," said Gudgeon.

"But," continued Masters, "say I was totally wrong about transshipping Hopcraft. That they intended to nab him and carry him off by vehicle from the very beginning. Fred, what does that suggest to you?"

Pollock stared at Masters for a moment and then said, "It could mean that they've kept him in this country the whole time. That he's still here, hidden away somewhere."

"That's what I think, and Bill agrees with me. He could still be within the UK. The question is where."

"Chief," said Reed, "I don't know how many million possible hiding places there are in this country, but it's so many that we don't stand a cat in hell's chance of finding Hopcraft without a massive, nationwide, police search. And that means letting the cat out of the bag good and proper."

"Quite right—on the face of it," replied Masters. "That is why, tomorrow, we are all going to be here, all day if necessary, going through every detail we know, from the very beginning, turning over and interpreting everything, in case we have missed anything or can wring out a further hint. Fred, you will be the moderator. You will preside and keep us on line, nominating speakers where necessary and generally making the whole thing coherent. I'd like you to think out your tactics between now and nine o'clock tomorrow morning."

"What about you, George? Won't you be here?"

"I shall be present, and will contribute in just the same way as everybody else. Under your guidance. I want your fresh mind in control."

"Fair enough. What about Moller and Berger?"

"We shall have to do without them. Berger rang in to say they had had no luck over tracing orders for equipment, but that Harry Moller had got some very faint hope in another direction. Naturally, he has to test it. They could rejoin us by tomorrow night."

Pollock said: "Right, gentlemen, nine o'clock here tomorrow morning. Sergeant Berger, I'd like you to make sure there's another table in here, and one more dining-chair. With paper for everybody to write on—if you haven't got it, buy it from a newspaper shop early tomorrow morning. And while you're at it, get a rubbish disposal sack to take waste paper so that we can get rid of it all safely. Bill, will you order water, orange juice and glasses to be waiting for us. We shall work until one o'clock and then break for one hour, so if anybody wants fags or mints to suck, see you bring them in with you."

6

Masters was very pleased he had asked Pollock to take over the duties of moderator.

The Truro man was strong and firm in running the review. He made notes as he went, calling on each member of the team to answer questions as he deemed necessary. Then he posed problems and asked for solutions from individuals, allowing others to come in when he thought they should be able to help. Only at intervals, when a suitable opportunity arose, would he allow a free-for-all for a limited time.

He went forwards, then backwards, to iron out inconsistencies or to square one fact with another. By lunchtime the problem was beginning to take coherent shape, like a rough lump of potter's clay that is beginning to show the outline of the vessel it is eventually to become.

When they broke up at one o'clock, Green said: "You're giving it some stick, Fred. I reckon we know it all backwards by now."

"It's the way forwards we're after," retorted Pollock. "And we haven't got there yet. But I'll tell you this. Your old mate George Masters hasn't lost any of his touch. The mere fact that he saw the need for, and then set up, this session shows that. It's dragging out of people ideas they never knew they had. Some good, some not so good. I mean, you take that one of young Reed's about the van: if all those old chaps were RASC soldiers who knew about vehicles, at least one of them should be able to tell us the make and by some means—hypnotism if need be—we could get the number out of them. It sounds far-fetched, but it's an idea. Then Gudgeon say-ing that we should try to trace back through Mrs Law-son's bank account the cheque that chap Juri settled his bill with—if he settled by cheque, that is. Not bad that, you know, for a man who's not a copper. And there have been more than a dozen like that. None immediately feasible, perhaps, but I've got 'em noted down. If all else fails we could try some of them."

"You don't have to convince me, Fred. I was here and heard it all. That's why I'm congratulating you on how you're running this seminar."

Masters came up to them. "I want to thank you, Fred, for doing so good a job. I know we're not in the clear yet, but at least I have the feeling that if there is an answer we should touch upon it here. But it's lunchtime. Come down and have a drink."

It was while they were standing in the residents' lounge that Masters was told there was an incoming call for him from Dr Moller.

"Put it through to my suite, please. I'll take it up there."

"Corn in Egypt, do you think?" Green asked Pollock. "I mean judging by the time of the call."

Gudgeon asked: "Are you trying to tell me that you can judge the contents of a call by its timing?"

"Not all calls," said Reed, "but this one probably. I mean, Sergeant Berger wouldn't ring the Chief during what he knows will be his lunchtime drinking break just to report failure. He'd save a bit of news like that till he got back. So if it's worth a long-distance call, it means something, even if it's only to ask the Chief for advice."

"That's right, lad," agreed Green, "and if they want advice, they want advice about something that's worth having advice about."

Gudgeon laughed. "You blokes! You can twist anything to mean what you want it to mean."

"Too true, Major," said Pollock. "I've had some of this lot before now. A year or two ago, in my manor. They had

156

me reeling, but it worked. And that's what everything we're doing today is about."

"And the longer the Chief's away," added Reed, "the more likely it is he's got a bite."

"Talking of bites," said Green, "where's the sarnies? I ordered a round of shrimp in mayonnaise and if I don't get it soon one of you lot'll have to buy me another drink to console me."

They had been settled to the sandwiches for several minutes before Masters rejoined them. "Where's my drink?" he asked. "Or did somebody finish it for me?"

"Aye, aye," said Green to Gudgeon. "We're making little jokes."

"A sign of good news?"

"You can bet your life on it."

Because of the veto on discussing the case in public, Masters said nothing until they reassembled at two o'clock in his suite. Then, after they'd all settled round the tables, he addressed Pollock. "With your permission, Fred, I'd like to make a report on the phone call I had from Harry Moller."

Pollock nodded his permission.

"I think we all know the value of having a scientist of Harry Moller's calibre with us on a venture such as this. When he first came down here and spoke to us about Hopcraft's work and the Rutland operation in general, he mentioned that certain pieces of specialized equipment had been designed by the Rutland chemical engineers and then constructed by a firm that deals with such things.

"That piece of information enabled me to hope that there could be something of value in exploring whether the specialist makers had been asked by anybody else for similar items of equipment. So I sent Moller and Berger off, only to be told last night that there had been no such requests which we could trace to source. So, as with various other ideas of mine, we were facing a blank wall in that direction.

"However, Moller had a further idea, linked in a way to the former one, but one which only he, as a scientist could have dredged up. It appears that besides buying individual pieces of equipment, Rutland had to buy in specialist substances.

"These substances, it appears, are called in the trade fine chemicals, as opposed to industrial chemicals. As their name implies they are one hundred per cent pure, or as near one hundred per cent as they can be made. Industrial chemicals are seventy-five or eighty per cent pure and are bought in bulk for all manner of purposes and processes. Fine chemicals are bought in very small amounts—comparatively speaking, that is—and are mainly for use in products such as drugs for human consumption.

"These fine chemicals, besides being purified, are very often highly complex, made up to complicated formulas which take professional handling and control. Their main purpose, I understand from Moller, is for use in the synthesis of other compounds.

"As you can imagine, people involved in research ask for individual fine chemicals to suit their books. Some, of course, are standard materials. But, as I've already said, they are usually supplied in quite small amounts.

"Rutland have been buying fine chemicals for Hopcraft's project. Some of them, I imagine, of their own devising—as opposed to standard substances. There are relatively few firms producing fine chemicals in the pharmaceutical world. Rutland were in the habit of buying all theirs from just one producer.

"Having failed over the special equipment area, Moller suddenly thought of fine chemicals. Of course, he had no idea of the substances Rutland were ordering, so he had to go back to them and ask for that information. They didn't like giving it to him and, indeed, they would not tell him all the formulas. But they finally gave him seven of the ten they use, together with the name of their supplier and a letter authorizing the supplier to answer questions about the supply and demand of those seven.

"Requests for single substances among the seven were of no use to Moller. Numerous firms could be taking one or two of them together, but he guessed that nobody except Rutland should be taking the full combination. And so, that is the question he put to the supplier when he and Reed arrived at the factory near Sheffield soon after midday today."

Masters looked round. "After ringing Rutland to confirm a few points, the fine chemicals people divulged that a firm calling itself The Retail Research Agency had, shortly before Christmas, asked for small supplies of chemicals which included the seven known to Moller, and four others, unspecified, three of which were normally provided to Rutland."

"They've cracked it, George," exulted Green.

"Not quite, Bill. As there were only small amounts of chemicals involved, the bill was a matter of a few hundred pounds. The order had been left by hand in the first place, and a representative of The Retail Research Agency collected the goods in person a few days later and paid on the spot in cash."

"And that didn't arouse suspicion?"

"Apparently not. Anyhow, there is neither address nor phone number for The Retail Research Agency."

"Bogus firm, of course."

"It would seem so."

"When are Moller and Berger due back?"

"They've been invited to lunch by the production director of the fine chemicals firm. He said he thought there would be several members of the scientific management in the party all anxious to bombard him with questions about his forensic work. It seems to have a fascination for those not involved in it, but knowing Harry Moller as I do, it wouldn't surprise me if he were to come away with more information than he has given out."

"DS Berger will be a bit out of his depth at a gathering like that, won't he?" asked Pollock.

"Obviously he won't be up to their weight in scientific

matters, Fred," replied Masters, "but lighter articles tend to float best. By that I mean he'll be the complete innocent among that crowd, asking apparently naive questions, and they'll probably fall over backwards to give him easily understood answers. And when that happens, replies are probably not so guarded as they might otherwise be. Berger, being a trained picker-up of nudges and winks could well find the experience useful not only to himself, but to us, too."

Pollock said: "Let's hope you're right. When can we expect them, then?"

Reed said: "From Sheffield to here is, I'd say, about a hundred and fifty miles, a lot of it motorway. The way DS Berger drives . . . well, they'll be here by six at the latest."

"Thanks, son," Pollock looked up. "Anything more to say on this particular development, George?"

"No. You all know as much as I do."

"Right. We'll get down to work then." He turned to Green. "Bill, I'd like you to give us your assessment of whether what we have just heard strengthens or weakens the theory that Hopcraft is still being held in the UK."

Green began. "We must get to know whether those particular fine chemicals can be obtained easily from some other country."

Pollock made a note.

Green went on logically. "Their bulk is important. If it were large, then they'd not be so easily transported abroad. If it is so small it can go in a diplomatic bag, for instance, the matter of sending them abroad presents no difficulty.

"If they are obtainable, say, in Germany, then I think that the fact they are bought here indicates Hopcraft could still be in the UK. If they are not available elsewhere, the question remains open because transport is so easy.

"I'd like to draw attention to the fact that no equipment has been bought here as far as we know. That suggests they are buying abroad from specialists in that field. It would be logical to suppose, therefore, that the fine chemicals are not available overseas. So I can't, at this stage, suggest that the purchase of fine chemicals in Sheffield points to Hopcraft still being in this country.

"Having said that, however . . ."

The session went on. Pollock made his notes, then probed and questioned, nominated speakers, invited views, stumped people, encouraged them, bullied them, all in an effort to get the last ounce of possibility out of their knowledge and flights of fancy.

At ten past four he said to Reed: "Ring for a tea trolley please, Sergeant." Then he said to Masters: "You will have come to your own conclusions as, indeed, will everyone else. I am—after I've had a cup of tea—going to write my findings up. The official moderator's conclusions. The copy will be distributed to each of you, in turn, for written observations. I shan't want essays. Maybe a yes will do for some sections. Only if someone disagrees will he be expected to put his reasons, briefly, in writing. I don't know how long all this will take, but I hope to reconvene here after dinner. Maybe at ten o'clock. So, after tea, the rest of you can clear out and get some fresh air while I do my stuff. Thereafter, Sergeant Reed will be responsible for circulating the file as quickly as possible. The file will only be accepted from, or handed to, Reed so that no time is lost."

Masters got to his feet: "Fred," he said, "I want to congratulate you on the way you have conducted today's proceedings. You did a marvellous job."

"And have you found it useful, George?"

"Immensely. Before even seeing your summary, I feel I can say I am encouraged to believe there are enough leads and suggestions to keep us moving. It could be a long haul, of course, but we could strike oil sooner than later."

Pollock looked gratified at the praise, but made no reply except to say, "I wish that char would come. I'm dying for a cuppa."

Masters, Green and Reed were walking abreast along the esplanade, taking the air that Pollock had suggested they should enjoy. It was already dark, but the wind had dropped to nothing more than a sea-breeze and, in consequence, the atmosphere was mild compared with that of the previous days.

"Where's Chas?" asked Green. "We haven't left him on his own have we?"

"No," replied Masters, "we're going to meet him."

"How do you mean going to meet him?"

"I hope, before not too many minutes have passed, we shall see him coming towards us."

"You mean he's gone home?"

"Actually, he's gone to see Mrs Lawson, at my request."

"Ah! You've latched on to that business about tracing that Juri bloke through the cheque he used to pay the rent for the cottage."

"That's it."

"You'd better tell us what you're thinking, George. Old Fred Pollock's sessions were a marvel. Quite honestly, I didn't think he had it in him to put us through the mangle quite so thoroughly. And he's achieved a lot by doing it. But I missed the informality of our usual sessions where we just meet to have a smoke, spit and swear. . . ."

"Me, too," said Reed, "but it's different this time, isn't it? For one thing there's the secrecy. Nobody can ask anybody a straightforward question. You have to put the question to yourself and then guess at the answer. And there's no focal point, like a dead body, or even knowing for sure whether we're looking for somebody in this country or anywhere else in the world, for that matter. Let alone whereabouts in this country he could be. We're fighting blind and in absolute silence."

"That about sums it up, lad," said Green. "You've virtually succeeded in telling us we haven't got a cat in hell's chance of pulling it off."

"I didn't say that. I meant our methods of tackling it have to be different—like the Chief ordering this council he had today and asking DCS Pollock to run it."

"Did you feel it did any good, Sergeant?"

"Yes, Chief. There were so many bits and pieces before. Now, if nothing else, it's all been pulled together. I know it looks as if the conclusion of the meeting will be that there's a lot of pretty boring routine ahead, following nothing but very slender leads, but it could all pay off in the end."

"Thanks," growled Green. "You're really making my day, lad."

"I think," said Masters, "that I detected movement ahead. Somebody crossed the road. . . ."

"It's the Major, Chief. He's crossed the grass, too. He's coming towards us."

In a few moments, Gudgeon was near enough to be recognized under the street lighting.

"Shall we just use this," said Masters, indicating a nearby shelter. "Then we can all talk in comfort."

"He paid in cash," said Gudgeon.

"Ah! Is that usual?" asked Masters.

"Beryl Lawson said it was most unusual, but then she usually gets a deposit by cheque when the booking is made and the balance, again by cheque, when the tenants arrive. Juri and his friends had not booked in advance, so they paid the whole whack at once when they moved in. Of course, Mrs Lawson didn't mind. In fact she was pleased. There was no risk of a dud cheque and . . ."

"And what, Charles?"

"I questioned her a bit on this point. Asked why a chap like Juri hadn't got a cheque-card and so on and she said he had. She actually saw it. One she didn't recognize. It was in his wallet when he took out the money. He paid in twenties and tens. She remembered because he made a joke about her preferring good English currency to a funny cheque. She thought he meant one that might bounce, of course, but my immediate thought was that he meant one drawn on a bank which wasn't one of the usual clearing banks. I mean, if the cheque-card was an unusual one, the cheque book, too, would be . . . well, to use Mrs Lawson's term, 'funny.'"

"Excellent, Charles. Thank you for that information.

"That sounds," said Green, "as though you like what you've heard. I thought you wanted to hear that Juri had paid by a cheque that could be traced."

"That was a possibility which I had hoped for," agreed Masters. "But what Charles has just said is almost as good as that. The average citizen of this country would regard the Bank of Cyrenaica as a 'funny' bank, don't you think?"

"Especially as Mrs Lawson caught a glimpse of a cheque-card that also looked funny. It probably looked odd because it had Arabic script all over it."

"Just so, Bill. We're guessing, of course, but Juri himself apparently used the description 'funny' to apply to his cheques. So what is a funny bank? There may well be scores of them in the City, but the Bank of Cyrenaica has figured already in the case, so I think we can safely assume that the two are one and the same. Two of them would be a bit much, I'd have thought."

"Agreed," said Green. "But where does it get us, except to confirm what we already know or suspect?"

"You heard what Sergeant Reed said a few minutes ago, about the long-protracted routine enquiries now facing us. He's right in his observation as things now stand. That, I believe, is what today's thrash has shown us. But apart from the fact that none of us likes lengthy routine enquiries, I don't believe we can afford the time to undertake them because they could involve months of work. In my opinion, neither Hopcraft nor Rutland has got that long."

"So what are you proposing to do?"

"Break out of the circle we are in now. I propose to go nap on one line of enquiry and say, 'This is it. This is what we must try to confirm. So we will concentrate on this aspect.'"

"And if you're wrong?"

"There are still the others to fall back on. But I feel we ought to start something, Bill, to get a reaction from the opposition if nothing else."

"I can't argue with that, but what particular flight of fancy have you got in mind?"

"I'll try to make this sound logical to you."

"Thanks."

"Charles has just heard that Juri paid in cash instead of using a funny cheque. Crease was seen speaking to a Libyan bank employee. We've agreed that the Bank of Cyrenaica links the two."

"Okay, so far."

"Harry Moller has reported that somebody else has handed over three or four hundred pounds in cash for chemicals rather than pay by cheque.

"On its own, cash payment isn't unusual. A new customer, wanting goods in a hurry, with no time to check bona fides and so forth. The chemical firm was probably very pleased at so considerate a way of doing quick business, and finance departments like accounts that are settled quickly so there is no need to send out invoices and reminders and so forth.

"As I say, it might have gone unremarked if a very similar method of payment hadn't been made under distinctly suspicious circumstances to Mrs Lawson. But now, I believe we can tie that transaction in with the other clues—in other words, with the Cyrenaican Bank.

"Three clues leading to that bank. Now, we are faced with finding a safe-house belonging to the Libyans, where they could be keeping Hopcraft if he is still in this country. Well, banks are safe houses, gentlemen. Nothing safer. They are built that way. . . ."

Green got to his feet. Masters looked up at him. "Have I disturbed you, Bill?"

"Yes you bloody well have."

"You think I have made a mistake?"

"You probably have. But you've . . . hell, George, vaults, cellars, living-quarters above, kitchens, loos, in fact everything there for keeping a man incarcerated, with underground space for him to work, in an area where nobody unconnected with the bank is allowed to go and where nobody expects to be able to go. And beautiful iron bars as good as a gaol to keep the prisoner in. And nobody suspects. Banks are above suspicion. They're places where. . . ."

"Propriety reigns?" queried Masters softly.

"If that's the word, yes."

"So you think we might be on to something, Bill?"

"Yes, blast it, I do. Now tell us how we're going to confirm it, or are you just proposing to walk in and ask for Hopcraft?"

"Both," replied Masters quietly. "It's ten to one that the bank, a new building, was intended to be all electric. But if Hopcraft needs bunsen burners, they'll have had gas put in, or they'll buy cylinders of butane. That shouldn't be hard to check. And they'll have to feed him, and not only him, but probably as many as two or three guards. We check whether the milkman's order has been increased these last few months, whether the baker has been delivering more bread. Oh, I needn't go on. With half a day's questioning in that area or at Fortnum's we could confirm whether or not Hopcraft is there. If we satisfy ourselves he is, we go in and ask for him."

"Just like that!"

"More or less. If they don't produce him . . . well, I think our masters will provide a cordon big enough to prevent anything getting into or out of that bank—certainly anything in the way of chemicals, equipment and the like. Even food."

"Starve 'em out?"

"And I doubt whether I shall have much difficulty in getting permission to tap their phones and intercept their mail, even though it could cause a diplomatic incident."

"You've got it all thought out, haven't you?"

"No, Bill. I'm sold on my own idea, obviously, but I wish I could think of some way to confirm it with no shadow of doubt. Just one pointer which says: 'This is it. Hopcraft is here.'"

"You want jam on it," retorted Green, "but there, I've always said you were jammy, so it wouldn't surprise me if you got three pounds of raspberry sent in the post tomorrow morning. And now, if nobody minds, I'm going back to the pub for a drink before dinner."

"I'll have to go, too," said Reed. "I've got to act as traffic clerk for Mr Pollock's file."

"We'll all go," said Masters. "Come along, Charles, and have a pre-dinner gin."

Moller and Berger joined them for the session in the bar before dinner. In accordance with Masters' instructions, no direct discussion of the case or reporting of events took place either then or at the dinner table, so nobody had heard their story in full until the meeting, which Pollock was able to reconvene at nine-thirty.

"I've read all your annotations on my written report," he began. "For the most part you have agreed that we have a true record of our deliberations and only here and there have you added notes to amplify what I put down. In your case, George, I see you have drawn together two points we appear to have missed, and that is that both the chemical company and Mrs Lawson were paid large amounts of money in cash and that this oddity is worthy of further discussion. I agree with that, though, to be frank about it, I wasn't aware that Mrs Lawson had been paid in cash."

"You weren't to know, Fred. It wasn't mentioned earlier, because it is a fact which has come to light since we broke up at teatime. Charles visited Mrs Lawson at my request to ask how she was paid."

"In the hope of tracing the cheque?"

"I thought it was a point that could be clarified while we were walking that way."

"Fair enough. But we'll take that up later if you don't mind. As the payment to the chemical company will form part of the report from the Doctor and Sergeant

Berger, I think it would be better if we had whatever information they can give us before we discuss the relationship between the two payments. In fact, in the light of what they say, we may wish to go over several other points."

"I agree that is the best procedure, Fred."

"Good. Now, everybody got beer or whatever drink they're having? Right, settle down please, gentlemen. Dr Moller, we'd like a factual report from you first, please, and inferences later."

Moller spoke of the first day when he and Berger had been unsuccessful in tracking down any other purchases of Rutland's specially designed equipment. Then he recounted how it had suddenly occurred to him that the Rutland laboratory, like any other research centre, would need refined chemicals for experimentation in an operation such as Hopcraft's. And, if he were any judge, a fair number of very complex chemicals.

He went on to say that, in his opinion, a knowledge of these formulas would not enable anybody to emulate the Rutland work, because the number of possible syntheses from so many complicated materials was vast. It would take a computer merely to work out the number of possibilities—and years of careful experimentation would be needed to exhaust those possibilities. So he returned to Rutland to try to persuade the director of research to let him know where the chemicals were specially put up and bought and, at the same time—in strict secrecy—to give him a list of formulas.

Rutland had not liked doing this, even though the chances of anybody being able to gain anything from the list were so small as to be negligible. But at last, the research director had written out in his own hand—after a visit to the laboratory—just seven of their ten formulas. He suggested that if any other person was buying a combination including those seven, he would be the person they were looking for.

Moller then opened his brief-case and put on the table a sheet of paper almost covered in chemical formulas.

"There you are, gentlemen. Seven formulas containing between them at least half of the symbols from the table of elements. Some are simply complex, some are complicated in manufacture because it is difficult to get some of the elements to combine with the others, or to do so in the ratios stipulated.

"That, however, need not concern us, which is just as well because I doubt whether we should any of us understand them fully, and some not at all if Sergeant Berger's reactions to them are anything to go by.

"We got back as far as Birmingham last night, and set out for Sheffield today after a breakfast before seven o'clock. The chemical company treated us extremely well. You must understand that they are not involved in secrecy to the same degree as Rutland, and they were quite willing to go as far as normal business confidentiality would allow. For, as one of them remarked to me, the formula for every drug used is widely publicized, so everybody who is interested can easily discover exactly who buys what in the way of chemicals.

"They willingly told me that the Retail Research Agency had bought not only the seven chemicals on the list, but the other three that Rutland bought regularly and one more which neither Rutland nor anybody else had ever asked for before.

"Bear in mind, gentlemen, that these chemical suppliers have no idea of the purpose for which Rutland buys these particular chemicals, so they saw no reason for not supplying a customer with a similar list. Sergeant Berger did a bit of questioning at this point, about the mechanics of the purchase. The Retail Research Agency, it appears, rang to ask if they could send a representative to drop in a list of their requirements and to receive assurance that the chemicals would, indeed, be available. So the RRA rep duly appeared with his written list and handed it over. He evidently expected to take the materials with him. He was told, however, that they would be several days in preparation and that they would be invoiced and sent on when ready. This did not appeal to him, apparently. He said he would call to collect the goods after an agreed four days, and would pay cash in order to show that he was not a man of straw.

"The list, this time, was a more comprehensive document than the one I have already shown you. I prevailed upon the company to give me a photocopy." He again opened his brief-case and this time took out a typewritten sheet. "You will note that it is typewritten—presumably so that nobody could possibly recognize Hopcraft's writing, should he have prepared it."

He put the sheet on the table. Masters picked it up to examine it as Moller continued to speak.

"The Rutland director who gave me the original list, simply scrawled the formulas for me. The one George is now looking at is annotated. By that, I mean one substance has the instruction 'sulphur free' alongside it. Another asks for 'analytical quality.' A third emphasizes 'ninety-nine per cent pure' and a fourth says 'limit of heavy metals one part per million.' These are all normal instructions that any research scientist would give to his supplier."

"Why are there eleven substances here, Harry?" asked Masters.

"I was just about to mention that anomaly. Rutland utilizes ten chemicals. Hopcraft—if it is Hopcraft—has asked for an eleventh. We were a little later back than we would otherwise have been because I took the precaution of checking with Rutland whether they had ever used the ion-exchange resin listed at number five. They said they had never ordered a chemical of that formula, but you can imagine they were more than interested to learn that somebody was proposing to use it in combination with the ten they have already established as those necessary in their processes.

"The suppliers were a little bemused by this extra item. They had never been asked for it before and consequently had to make it from the beginning. This was not basically complicated, they said, except that the ingredients were a little difficult to make stick together.

The list is actually annotated as to the method to be used for making the substance, but the chemical company could not find the reference, and so had to use their own method.

"As I said, they managed it, and the goods were handed over to the Research rep when he called. He paid in cash, which the firm did not object to, especially with a new and unknown customer. You don't get bad or out-standing debts doing business that way.

"And that, gentlemen, is the full story. I personally believe the list came from Hopcraft via his captors, but I cannot, obviously, swear that it tells us whether he is in this country or Libya, let alone his whereabouts within either country."

"Thank you, Harry," said Pollock. "Now. . ."

"One moment, please, Fred," said Masters.

"Something strikes you?"

"Yes. Harry, did you say the chemical firm could not find the reference to the extra chemical?"

"That's correct. And it seems rather odd, because firms of that stature usually have all that sort of thing readily available to them."

Masters stood up and placed the paper in front of Pollock. "With your permission, Fred, I would like the others to gather round to read the item we are talking about."

The others looked over the shoulders of the two detective superintendents as Masters pointed to the fifth request on the list.

Ion-Exchange Resin loaded as follows:
BA-1%; N-1.5%; K-5%, according to the method
of Marisk and Kirchstrasse, Monatschrift
fur Brass und Chemie 26: 5; 72 (1981)

"What about it?" demanded Moller. "It is a perfectly normal way of identifying a fine chemical."

"My German is a bit rusty," admitted Masters, "but I do know what Kirchstrasse means in English. It means

171

Church Street. I also know that the word marish is an old English word for marsh, so I imagine that marisk means the same in German. And a marsh, gentlemen, would be one way of describing a fen."

"Fenchurch Street," growled Green. "You've got the bastard, George. It's a bogus reference that Hopcraft made up. That's why it couldn't be found."

"I think so. I know no such word as brass in German. I think our friend Hopcraft is referring to the purchase of the chemicals for brass or, in other words, cash." He looked up. "But I think what clinches it, gentlemen, is the formula. Forget the percentages and the other verbiage, and what do you get? Barium, Nitrogen and Potassium: Ba, N, K—Bank."

"Bank, Fenchurch Street?" asked Moller.

"Sorry, Harry," replied Masters. "You are probably not fully aware . . . look, I'll put you in the picture."

Masters gave a brief outline of the conversation during which it had been suggested that the Bank of Cyrenaica was being used as a safe house by Hopcraft's captors.

"And I didn't spot that clue from the list of formulas," moaned Moller. "Neither did Rutland, nor the chemical firm. But once pointed out, it's as plain as pikestaff. A difficult, hitherto unknown formula with a bogus reference. And to cover the fact that he needed to annotate that one, he annotated the others so as not to rouse suspicion. George, if ever I wore a hat, I'd raise it to you."

Pollock said: "Sit down, gents, please." He turned to Masters. "There's no point in going on trying to find an answer we've already got, George. But we still have to get hold of Hopcraft. Do you want to discuss ways and means of doing that?"

"Yes, please, Fred. And, if I may, I'd like to re-emphasize at this juncture the need for secrecy. More than ever now. If they were to get wind of our success, his captors would spirit Hopcraft away—alive or dead. I do not think they would have the slightest hesitation in killing him in an effort to prevent our ever getting to know exactly what has happened and what they are planning for the future."

"Meaning, I take it," said Pollock, "that we are still on our own."

"That is what our masters would want."

"So we are to discuss a plan which involves us alone?"

"Yes."

"Five of us?"

"Five?" demanded Moller. "Seven."

Masters said: "It's a police job, Harry."

"Nuts," retorted Moller. "I've been officially appointed part of this team. You will need me to look over any laboratory they may have set up for Hopcraft."

"And me," said Gudgeon. "I'm probably the best qualified of anybody here if there's going to be any nonsense."

Green said: "It looks as if you've got a mutiny on your hands, George."

Masters grinned. "I can hardly call volunteers mutineers, Bill."

"Not in your present mood, you can't," conceded Green. "I don't feel too bad about it all, myself, but you . . . well, the weight has lifted, hasn't it? I mean you're grinning like a riven dish and you haven't done much of that these past few days."

Gudgeon said: "After deciphering the message in that formula, I should think he has every reason to feel happy." He turned to Masters. "Good work, that. Congratulations."

"Thank you, Charles. Now, I'd like to get on, Fred, because I hope we shall leave here tomorrow with some idea of how to proceed up in London."

Pollock called the meeting to order, and then said to Gudgeon, "This won't be an overt police operation. If it were, the bank would be surrounded by armed police and newsreel cameras would be letting all the world and his wife know what we were up to. It's got to be low-key, Major. Nobody must know. You're the planning officer. What do you propose?"

Gudgeon hesitated a moment or two before replying. Then: "I should want to know several things. First, do they ever take Hopcraft out of the building? If they do, do they use any regular route? Everybody here will realize it will be easier to rescue Hopcraft in the open air—given the chance.

"If observation says he is never taken out, then I want to know the lay-out of the bank and, if possible, get some idea of whereabouts within it Hopcraft is kept.

"To do this we can either find a similar building and reconnoitre that, or we can find the architects and ask to see the plans."

"Copies of plans are always deposited with one of the departments in the GLC," murmured Reed. "We could get an official view of those without rousing suspicion, perhaps."

Gudgeon continued. "Observation must be kept at all exits, to see if there are guards who go on in shifts or come out at night for a pint. Important, this, because we shall have to decide on the best time to go in. Opening time in the morning? Just on closing time in the afternoon? Force a guard returning at night to let us in? The possibilities and alternatives may be quite numerous. Personally, I favour evening or night, when not only the bank but the whole of Fenchurch Street will be pretty quiet."

"There's always traffic to and from London Bridge," said Berger.

"We could fix that," said Green. "They close the bridge often enough. We could get it done to suit us and divert the traffic if needs be."

"Then the plan inside," went on Gudgeon. "There'll be alarms to be silenced and the occupants to be rounded up, for which we shall need to be armed. After that it is a matter of locating keys and opening up doors." He turned to Pollock. "To write an operation order for that will take time, because it will have to be based on the information we get from plans and observation. I know banks are robbed almost daily, but this is a differ-

174

ent proposition. We're not going in there to grab money from the till and then roar away inside two minutes. We've got to locate a man and get him away safely. And it is no use thinking we can break in at a weekend from the next-door premises, because if Hopcraft is there, the bank won't be unoccupied at weekends, which is the usual proviso for such exploits."

Pollock nodded. "Thank you, Major. You've given us a brief idea of what we shall have to do, and the difficulties involved." He turned to Green. "Bill, let's hear from you concerning what the Major has said."

Green shrugged. "They say that poachers make the best gamekeepers, but not the other way round. We're gamekeepers and always have been. For the likes of us to break into a bank is, to my way of thinking, asking for trouble in a big way. It's all right for Chas. He's been trained for such capers, but I haven't and I'm a bit long in the tooth for bullet dodging. The doc won't even know what it's about. You other four could perhaps make a show of it, but I doubt it. It's not our form."

"So what is your suggestion?"

"That George should report to the big boss and ask for trained help. The SAS if needs be. A small, secret operation."

"Secret?" asked Reed. "With stun bombs going off in a bank and canisters puthering out clouds of smoke from every window and door? That's the way the SAS do it. Very effective it is, too. But it can't be kept quiet."

"They can operate stealthily," objected Gudgeon. "With knives and life-preservers and such."

"And if the guards are armed and start shooting?" asked Moller. "There'd be bangs a-plenty then. And I suspect that even in stealthy operations the SAS carry guns in case the need to use them arises. I reckon there'd be a very noisy battle."

Gudgeon grimaced. "Of course you have to send the chaps in fully armed. They'd be at a disadvantage otherwise."

"What do you think, George?"

Masters, thus appealed to, said: "I think there's a lot in what Bill Green has said. And I must report to our masters tomorrow. But my opinion is that they'll fight shy of bringing in any form of troops and will want us to do the job. Charles has very rightly pointed out some of the difficulties, but I want us to find a way if one exists. Please don't forget the diplomatic side of this and the repercussions there could be if we don't manage it quietly and sensibly. Could we, therefore, please turn our minds to more subtle approaches."

"Like what?"

"Could we lure them out? Fake messages telling them to move Hopcraft to a house in the country? Or could we kidnap one or two of their people and demand Hopcraft as a ransom? Put knock-out drops in the milk so that they are all comatose when we go in?" He spread his hands. "There are probably hundreds of such schemes or combinations of them which we could think up. So can we try that approach, please, Fred?"

"I like it," replied Pollock. "Sarn't Berger, you heard what the Chief said. I'd like some thoughts from you on the subject."

Berger leaned forward. "What we may or may not be able to do in this area will depend on what we can discover about the habits of the bank staff. Observation has been mentioned by the Major. Earlier, I think I heard mention of tradespeople who supply the bank. I think we should try to build up a picture of their lifestyle in detail. The Chief mentioned doping the milk. But we've got to get at the milk. What I mean is, is it likely to be left on the front doorstep? Or do we have to nobble the local shopkeeper? There are hundreds of things. . . ."

The meeting went on until Pollock called a halt at one o'clock. The only things that had been definitely decided were that they should clock out of the Water's Edge Hotel the next morning and head for London, with Pollock to become a guest in the Green household and Gudgeon in that of Masters and his wife. This disposition had been decided because neither Green nor Gudgeon had a car and Masters preferred to have a vehicle at each house. Moller had his own car in London, while the sergeants could draw from the yard pool if the need arose.

As Green, who was last to leave the suite, was saying goodnight to Masters, he said: "Those dispositions are correct, George, but I'd prefer to travel up with you if you don't mind. You never know, there might be something we want to talk over."

"I agree, Bill. Pollock won't mind taking Moller and Gudgeon. We'll sort ourselves out at the other end."

7

As Reed drove the Yard Rover towards London the next morning, Masters said, "My great fear, Bill, is that Hopcraft is not being held in that bank."

"You what?"

"That we should make some move against the lives of not exactly friendly aliens, but not ostensibly enemy, and their property, and then discover that Hopcraft is not there."

"Come off it, George. You deciphered that message. It was plain to all of us once you'd pointed it out that he said he was being held in a bank in Fenchurch Street. And The Bank of Cyrenaica is in Fenchurch Street."

"True enough. He was there when he wrote the order for chemicals and concocted his message to include in it. But that was some time ago. The parcel was made up before Christmas. He could have been moved before now. We may not be always as successful as we'd like to be in policing the realm, but I have a suspicion that many of our foreign friends credit us with being more adept at stopping their little games than are most of our colleagues in other countries. That being so, the people who have Hopcraft could well have thought it wise to keep him on the move, just in case we started getting a line on them, or alternatively, they could have moved him overseas."

"No," said Green, positively. "I'm not wearing either of those suppositions. And I'll tell you why. First off, you have told us—and I believe you— that there is no reason for the Libyans to suppose that we link them in any way with Hopcraft's disappearance. Right?"

"Absolutely right. Until this week I have worked alone and I have gone nowhere near anybody connected with the Libyans."

"They've had Hopcraft for months now, without a word to connect them with his disappearance. That means they must be feeling safe. For anybody in a safe position to start moving a captive about this country or to attempt to smuggle him out is asking for trouble. That is when they would run into the danger they had avoided up to then, so why court trouble?"

"That's a good point," said Berger.

"Thanks for the support, lad," said Green before continuing. "As you said, a bank is a safe place. They'd know it was better to keep Hopcraft there than at some building like that Libyan People's Bureau they used to have instead of an embassy. Places like that have an eye kept on them by Robby Lippert and his mates. I'll bet they don't watch banks half as much."

"That could well be true," conceded Masters.

"And if we know it, they know it. That's why they mounted the snatch from there and took Hopcraft there immediately after they'd lifted him." Green paused for a moment. "They'd prepared for him, George, or have done so since. They've set him up there with a laboratory. Must have done if they're getting chemicals for him. They won't want to be moving laboratories hither, thither and yon. Too tricky. Equipment getting broken, things going wrong and being lost, to say nothing of the interruption it would be to the work he's supposed to be doing for them. I always thought you couldn't interrupt these chemical experiments without having to start all over again?"

"That is generally accepted as being the case."

"So they haven't moved him—anywhere. He's still in the vault of that bank. And I haven't forgotten, either, that late yesterday afternoon, before we'd got the mes-

179

sage Hopcraft had hidden in the formula, you were bending my ear about breaking the vicious circle and going out on a limb bald-headed. You even chose that bank as your first objective. Now I'm not suggesting that anything you said then is evidence to support my contention that Hopcraft is still in the bank. But I am saying it was your instinct that made you choose the bank as your first target for investigation, and I'm old-fashioned enough to believe in instinct when a bloke like you is as fully steeped in a case as you are in this one. The something-or-other, what's the word? Spontaneity? Yes, that's it. The spontaneity of instinct gives it a sort of edge which is blunted by too much thinking about things."

"The DCI's right, Chief," said Reed, keeping his eyes firmly on the road ahead. "Those Libs are working away in blissful ignorance. Why the hell should they change what they think is a winning game?"

"Where are we stopping for lunch?" demanded Green, changing the subject completely, as though the matter had finally been settled.

"I didn't know we were going to stop," said Reed.

"You mean you didn't arrange with those other boyos to join us at some pub?"

"Never thought of it."

"Then you should have done. Fred Pollock owes me a drink. If he doesn't show up you'll have to buy it."

"Why me?"

"Because you didn't make the arrangements."

"Doc Moller owes me a drink, if it comes to that, but I notice you made no arrangement on my behalf."

"You mean you are refusing to stand surety for Mr Pollock's debts?"

"And for your liquid assets."

"In that case, I'll have to see him myself."

"Which should be in about half an hour," said Masters. "I've agreed with him we'll meet up at the King's Head, to sort ourselves out. You know it, Reed. Past Reading and . . ."

180

"I know the one, Chief. I gave DCS Pollock the instructions for getting there."

"Acting the fool were you, lad?" growled Green. "Just for that you can buy me my second drink and you might as well add a ploughman's to your bill while you're at it."

"In a pig's ear," retorted Reed.

All Wanda Masters knew about her husband's current case was that it had taken him to Yourhead. From there he had phoned her each evening but she had learnt nothing more than that the weather was foul for most of the time and that he had met Fred Pollock who she had also met several times a couple of years earlier in Blumaryon and Truro.

Then this morning had come another call asking her to prepare for a guest in the little house behind Westminster Hospital. The name had surprised her. Not a police officer, but a Major Charles Gudgeon, but the name rang a distant bell with her. She had tried to recall in what circumstances she had heard the name before, but the memory eluded her.

Shortly after three, Reed nudged the big Rover down the narrow road to the house.

"Darling, this is Charles Gudgeon. We've merely dropped in to leave our bags and to let Charles make his number. He is, as they say, helping us with our enquiries—but in the nicest possible way. He and I have to go on to the Yard for an hour or so, but we should be back by . . . well, I'd guess before five."

After kissing her husband and smiling at Reed, Wanda shook Gudgeon's hand. "Welcome to our home, Major Gudgeon. We shall do all we can to look after you while you're here, but I'm afraid our spare bedroom is quite small. We have such a tiny house. . . ."

"About as big as mine, I'd say, ma'am, so I'm sure I shall feel perfectly at home." He looked round him at the little hall and through to the dining-room which ran right across the rear of the building. "And I must say

181

you have a jewel here. Bill Green told me he calls it Wanda's Palace, and he wasn't far wrong."

"How is William?"

"Fine," replied her husband. "He should be home by now. He and Doris are going to entertain Fred Pollock for a few days. But we'll tell you all about it later. We must get off now."

Masters left Gudgeon in his office in Reed's care, while he himself sought an interview with Anderson, the AC Crime and, after him, with the Commissioner.

The Commissioner listened quietly while Masters made his report, making it as brief as possible while still giving the great man the necessary evidence to back up the facts.

"I agree with Green," said the Commissioner. "The man has to be at the bank. And you've got to get him out, Masters. With no fuss. I shall report to the Home Office myself, but from what I have already heard, they will not sanction the use of troops or even a body of our own men unless the need becomes imperative. It will not become imperative in their eyes unless and until you have tried and failed."

"Have you any thoughts on the matter, sir?"

"Only to emphasize that whatever you do must be low-key. Further, I want no violence on our side if it can be avoided. You have this Gudgeon man with you. Can he be relied upon to act with circumspection? He sounds to be a bit trigger-happy?"

"I regard him as entirely reliable, sir. His record would suggest he is a bit quick off the mark, but on both the occasions when it has happened he has been in extreme danger and his reactions are those of a man I would like to have by my side."

"I'll take your word for it. I've said no violence on our side, but that doesn't mean I want casualties on our side, either. You have my permission to draw arms for your men should you think them necessary. And by necessary, I mean should there be the slightest need for them. These people you are up against have no scruples, Masters. So take no risks. No risks whatsoever. Having said that, I leave it to you and this other DCS. Pollock, is it? Good luck, Masters, and make it as soon as you can. I don't like this sort of thing hanging over us."

Masters got to his feet to leave the office but the Commissioner waved him back to his seat.

"You think I've not given you much direct help, George. It's not because I'm unwilling to do so, but because to do so would be something of an impertinence on my part. You are the man in charge and the man who knows every detail of the case. Quite frankly, for me to step in now might be more of a hindrance than a help." He sat back in his chair. "I wasn't too happy about this particular chore being handed to the police—members of my force or any other. But the opinion of our masters was that policemen would be better at following up normal clues and investigating the disappearance of this man, Hopcraft, than would, say, our Intelligence brethren. So much is true. Tracing missing persons is our job. And if it comes to that, so is dealing with thugs and villains. But by and large, being an accountable service, we prefer to work overtly. We have to maintain secrecy, of course, but usually only when it concerns our own actions in the investigation of crime. Political secrecy—if I may call it that—or, as in this case, political secrecy with international undertones, and hence the possibility of diplomatic repercussions—should properly, in my opinion, be left to our more secret organizations. But it was felt that they, though intensely subtle in most of their undertakings, are not necessarily governed quite so strictly as we are by the rule of law and they tend to settle their problems themselves. What I mean by that is that where we have to put our headaches in front of judge and jury, they are not so inhibited. I hate to suggest that they employ a surfeit of hit-men—in this country at any rate—but they do have facilities for removing encumbrances that we do not possess. And this colours their activities, George. Where the likes of us need continuity of evidence to prove our cases, they can identify theirs without evidence and dispose of them as they see fit.

"And I, personally, thought that this could well become a case for such treatment. Hence my dislike of it having been handed to the police. So far, apparently, you have proved our masters right and justified their faith in you. But now the scenario has changed, George. You may now be required to act contrary to the law of the land, in circumstances so secret that you are virtually denied the protection of those who are ordering you to do it. I, for one, would not be allowed to speak out in your defence, should you need it. And if not me, who? Put not your trust in politicians and their underlings, George. Their careers are more important to them than yours. So tread warily, and use that brain of yours to concoct a watertight cover story, so that if a storm should break you've got an umbrella right above your head and firmly in your grasp."

After a moment or two of silence, Masters said quietly: "Thank you, sir. Events will prove me right or wrong, as the case may be. But what you've just said will, I believe, help me a great deal in deciding how to proceed."

"If that's so, I'm glad. I'm afraid I ran on a bit, but I'm the onlooker here. And not only that, I feel a great responsibility for you and your team though, technically, I am supposed to be totally unaware of your activities." He got to his feet. "Now, you'd better go. And the best of luck. I hope you can finish the job as well as you've started it."

When Masters reached his own office, Reed said: "DCS Pollock phoned, Chief. He'd like to know if you want to see him and DCI Green again this evening."

"Please ask Mr Pollock if the two of them will join me at my house at half past eight this evening. You and Berger and Dr Moller too, if he's free. Oh, and please include Mrs Green in the invitation. If she's willing to come she can keep my missus company for an hour or so while we talk. I'm taking Major Gudgeon off now. I shall take it that everybody will be present, so you need only ring me if there is some snag."

184

"Right, Chief. See you at half eight."

"Darling," said Wanda, as they sat down for supper, "Charles has been telling me about his cottage."

"It's a delight, my poppet. There's a row of them, some of which are to let as holiday homes. Whether they compare with Charles's home I can't say, but having seen his I thought I would mention them to you as a possible holiday spot for us. You'd enjoy being so near the sea, and Michael would like the beach. Best of both worlds there. Sea and country."

"You really think we'd like it?"

"I do, and I only saw it in a gale."

Wanda turned to Gudgeon. "You were right, Charles. And it was awfully sweet of you to invite us to stay with you, but I think it would be better if we were to ask Mrs Lawson if we might hire one of her properties."

"Too late, my dear," replied Gudgeon. "She's fully booked. And even if she wasn't, it's ten-to-one she wouldn't have vacancies at the time you'd want to come. No, you join me. There's as much room for four as you've got here and I'd be delighted to have you. I mean that. Delighted. And the boy. He's a great little chap. I'd have liked one like him for myself. Pick your time, and come for a family fortnight."

"Are you really sure? It sounds gorgeous . . . George, what do you think?"

"I've told you, sweetheart. We'd enjoy Yourhead. If Charles is prepared to put up with us. . . ."

"That's settled then," said Gudgeon. "I'm already looking forward to your visit. Once we get this present problem out of our hair, we can get down to planning the holiday."

"What is the present problem?" asked Wanda. "I know nothing of it, though George usually gives me some idea of his big cases."

Masters replied before Gudgeon could speak. "It's an abduction case, poppet. Chap was kidnapped down in Yourhead. We've established he's now being held up

185

here, somewhere, but we're keeping more than average quiet about it because we don't want his captors to know we're on to them. It could jeopardize the man's life. So I've told everybody to say nothing about anything. And having given Bill and the sergeants those strict instructions, I must obey them myself. And that, my darling, is as much as I'm prepared to say at the moment, except that Charles here helped us a lot down in Yourhead and I called on Fred Pollock because he's knowledgeable about the south-west of the country. We hope to finish up within the next few days."

Wanda smiled. "Thank you. I've been wondering, because it's not like you to be secretive, but if you've laid strictures on the others, you've got to toe your own line. Now, coffee? Black or white, Charles?"

The meeting was a short one. Masters reported on his meeting with the Commissioner and confessed that the conversation had, in fact, helped him to make up his mind how to act. For his plan to succeed he needed certain information. For instance, he had to ascertain whether the man Juri, who had rented Mrs Lawson's cottage, worked at the bank and whether that was his real name. He gave this task to Pollock and Gudgeon, with instructions to photograph the man and to get Mrs Lawson's identification of him if possible. Green, Berger, Reed and Moller were to concentrate on the bank. Their job was to discover its layout and to keep observation as to the comings and goings of customers and staff in an effort to determine the best time of entry and the best dispositions within the building should a team need to enter. He gave them four days in which to achieve their objectives.

"That takes us to Monday evening, gentlemen, so the observers will have the benefit of seeing what goes on at the bank over the weekend. From time to time I may ask for reports and may give further instructions, but so that you are all in the picture as to what I propose, here is the outline of my plan."

Masters continued to speak for only a few more minutes and then ended the meeting with an invitation for all of them to join the ladies for a drink.

"I don't like it, George," said Green, stubbornly, before they had chance to leave the dining-room where they had been talking. "It could be dangerous. You don't know the place. It's not like a British High Street bank. No bullet-proof windows at the counters. Just bronze grills with holes in them the size of saucers and all shaped like those onions. . . ."

"Onions?"

"Onion-shaped domes."

"I see."

"No you don't. I tell you it's dangerous."

"Can you suggest a plan that won't have an element of danger, Bill?"

"No, I can't, but. . . ."

"Sorry, Bill. That's it."

Green shrugged. "It's your funeral — or could be, literally."

They met again on Monday evening. Pollock and Gudgeon, who in between times had journeyed back to Yourhead with a photograph, assured Masters that Juri worked at the bank and had been observed coming and going that day. Moller produced a copy of the architect's plans and briefed them on these. He had, he confessed, entered the bank on the heels of another customer and had used one of the tables, ostensibly, for the purposes of writing a cheque and a short letter while taking in the scenery first hand. Green produced a detailed list of times and customer-flow and gave his considered opinion as to the best time to enter the bank.

Eleven forty was his suggested time.

At exactly eleven forty the next morning, Masters entered the Bank of Cyrenaica, holding a large envelope. He was unarmed.

He had split his force. Pollock was outside, with Berger and Moller. Some seconds after Masters entered the bank, Green, Reed and Gudgeon followed individually. All were armed.

Conscious of the television cameras that watched his every move, Masters approached the counter while Green and Gudgeon stopped halfway between it and the door, as though to chat. Reed went to the left to use the table formerly used by Moller. He carried a brief-case, put it on the table and opened it up to take out a sheaf of papers.

"I would like to speak to Mr Juri, please."

The young Libyan behind the counter said: "Mr Juri doesn't see people without an appointment."

"Please tell him I am a police officer." Masters showed his identity card.

The youth stepped away from the counter to use a phone on one of the tables where girls were flicking through cheques and using adding machines. Masters could not be sure about it, but over the noise he thought he could hear a distant bell ringing insistently. He glanced round. It seemed Green had heard it, too.

The youth put his hand over the mouthpiece of the phone and said: "Mr Juri would like to know the nature of your enquiry, sir."

"Please tell him it concerns forged bank notes which we believe may have passed through his hands."

The youth turned again to the phone. It was then that a door to the side of a flight of stairs on the staff side of the counter opened. The sound of the bell was now louder, so much so that Masters glanced that way. He was aware of the figure coming half through the door; aware even that the man was armed. And then the bullet took him, high on the left arm. Despite the searing pain he was aware that the first man had dodged behind the counter to be followed by a second armed figure. And then more guns spoke. A brief chatter of shots. He saw Green standing beside him. The girls and the youth on the floor behind the counter. Reed moving cautiously, Smith and Wesson at the ready. Gudgeon, his gun still held at the firing position saying to nobody: "That was Farries, and I got the bastard."

"Shut the door," said Masters. "Bill, you and Reed look for Hopcraft."

Pollock appeared before Gudgeon could shoot the bolts.

"Hold them off, Fred," said Masters. "You know the cover story. Get an ambulance. There are two dead villains here."

"You're hurt, George."

"Painful but hardly serious, I think. Send Berger in, would you. I want those two bodies brought this side of the counter. Hurry man. All the world and his wife will be here in a minute."

The evening papers and news programmes carried the story, culled from a police handout. The police had surprised two armed robbers actually in the process of robbing the bank. The thieves had been armed and had opened fire on the police. In the exchange of shots DCS Masters of Scotland Yard had been wounded. The two robbers had both been shot dead by the police. The police had failed to capture a third robber, who had been in the get-away car. At the first sound of shots he had sped towards Aldgate and was then lost. The police believed they knew his identity and were already searching for him.

Nowhere was there a mention of Hopcraft.

Pollock and Green had dealt with Juri and other senior members of the bank staff. It was the script which had been prepared by Masters during the preceding few days.

"You know and we know," said Pollock, addressing them collectively, "that you abducted Dr Hopcraft and have been holding him, against his will, incarcerated in this bank. We also know that as soon as a senior police officer came to speak to you, Juri, you panicked and alerted the villains you had hired to guard Dr Hopcraft.

189

"We've been on to you for some time. We know how you, Juri, contacted the dead villain Crease. We know how you and Farries, with the woman Barcurata, rented a cottage in Yourhead and how, using that as a base, you abducted Dr Hopcraft while he was on his walking tour.

"You were right to panic, Juri. But you were wrong to invite Crease and Farries to see DCS Masters through your television cameras and then to allow them to gun for the Chief Superintendent. The DCS was unarmed himself, but he was backed up by marksmen.

"I'm here to tell you that not one word of what actually happened here today is to get out. Your junior staff think it was a bank raid. And that is what it will be regarded as by you and everybody else. Farries and Crease were known criminals. They had got into your bank to rob it and they had panicked when they realized Mr Masters was on the premises, even though he had come about some totally different matter. Forged banknotes to be precise. Fortunately, Mr Masters' companions happened to be armed, and after the DCS had been wounded they opened fire and killed the gunmen.

"Your bank has lost nothing. You will not mention Dr Hopcraft, otherwise the world will be told of your activities and some of you people will find yourselves in British gaols for many a long year.

"That's the way it is going to be. You lot are getting off scot-free in the interest of relations between this country and yours. There are some people—among them me—who would like to teach you Libyans a lesson. Don't give us the excuse we need by departing—by as much as a single word—from what I have just told you.

"Any questions?"

There were no questions.

"Right. You can open for business as soon as Dr Moller and those working with him tell you they have removed all Dr Hopcraft's papers and equipment."

Green opened the door of Masters' small house before Doris was out of the car.

"After you phoned," she gasped, "it was on the news. Sergeant Reed hasn't told me anything in the car except that George has been hurt. Where's Wanda? Where's Michael?"

Green sought to quieten her. "Come in. Reed has to get back to help look after things. I've made a pot of tea. I'll pour you a cup."

"Where's Wanda?"

"She's just across the way at the hospital. I had George brought to the Westminster so that she could pop in and out. Michael is here, in the sitting-room. He's drawing."

"You're looking after the little pet?"

"Why not? I'm his godfather."

"Have you given him his lunch?"

"No. I was waiting for you to do that, but I gave him a glass of milk to tide him over. Wanda said there was something ready for him in the fridge. It just needs heating up. A small fish pie and green beans, I think she said, and some stewed apricots which he eats cold."

"Right. I'll just see to that, then I'll want to know exactly what's been going on."

"Sorry, love, I've got to push."

"Not before you tell me what I want to know." She lit the gas oven and put the small Pyrex dish of fish pie on to a baking tray. She waited to make sure the flame was completely alight and then put the tray in. As she closed the door, she went on: "Why was George shot at?"

"He went into the bank to make official enquiries about some forged bank notes. Two villains were inside and recognized him. They were armed, so they started shooting. George stopped one."

"He hadn't a gun?"

"No."

"But there were armed police there. They shot the gunmen."

"Yes."

"You were there, weren't you? And Fred Pollock and the sergeants."

"Yes."

"What other policemen were with you?"

"None. Just Charles Gudgeon and Dr Moller."

She stared at him.

"So if there were no other police there, it was you others who were carrying guns."

Green nodded.

Doris grew angry. "So George knew there was going to be trouble. Expected it, or else he wouldn't have issued guns to you others." She stamped her foot. "I never thought George would be so irresponsible."

"How d'you mean, love?"

"To go marching into a bank unarmed when he expected people to shoot at him. He could have been killed."

"So?"

"So he was irresponsible. He must have known he could have left Wanda a widow and little Michael fatherless, yet he went in there without taking any precautions. It was criminal of him, and I shall tell him so."

Green looked at her steadily for a moment and then placed both his hands on her shoulders.

"Dolly," he said quietly, "you know what I think of you. What we've meant to each other all this time?"

"Of course I do. What's that got to do with it?"

"This. If ever you breathe one word of what you've just been saying to Wanda and George, you and I will be finished."

"You what? Bill Green, I. . . ."

"Listen, Dolly. Do you honestly believe that a bloke like George didn't think of those things, or that he would ever act in any way to prejudice the happiness of Wanda and Michael without an overwhelming reason?"

"I wouldn't have done before today. Besides, what bigger reason for not risking your life could there be than your wife and child? I. . . ."

"The lives of hundreds of thousands. Maybe millions. Yes, you can open your eyes in disbelief, old girl, but that was what George was faced with. You'll not get to hear the full story for years, if ever. But George knew the dangers, and he also knew that he had to be able to say he was unarmed and didn't provoke the shoot out. As a matter of fact, he did, because somebody had to, and George isn't the sort to send anybody else into danger—me, for instance—when he could take the risk himself. He wasn't irresponsible. He took all the precautions he could by having Reed and myself there with guns, and Charles Gudgeon, who's an ex-SAS man, along as well. As I say, you'll probably never hear the full story. Anything you hear, in fact, will be a cover-up. But take it from me, George was thinking of Wanda and Michael and thousands like them. So don't ever hint to Wanda that he was acting irresponsibly and jeopardizing her happiness and his son's future, because it isn't true."

"You mean he actually manufactured a situation by presenting himself as a target for gunmen?"

"That was one of the possibilities. If he'd been a bit luckier there wouldn't have been any shooting."

"And if he'd been a bit unluckier, there wouldn't have been any George."

Green smiled. "I think I can smell the nipper's food cooking. Best look at it before it burns."

"Oh, my goodness!" As she reached for the oven cloth she looked up at him. "Bill, you haven't called me Dolly since we were courting."

"We're still courting," her husband replied. "Courting trouble. We're not out of the wood yet."

Wanda clung to his free arm. "You fool! Oh, you fool!" she said, her voice shaky with a mixture of fear and thankfulness.

He hadn't a hand to put round her or with which to caress her. With difficulty, because she showed no intention of loosening her hold, he lowered his head to kiss the top of her hair. "I can hardly be called a fool," he objected jocularly, "if I walk into a bank and a villain takes a shot at me."

She drew her head back and looked up at him.

"Why were you there?"

"On police business. Forged notes, actually."

"Were you armed?"

"No."

"But you must have been expecting trouble otherwise the others wouldn't have been carrying guns."

"There was a possibility of trouble. Just a hint."

"And you went in defenceless."

"I didn't want to start any nastiness."

"I don't understand."

"Bill, Charles and Sergeant Reed were there to protect me—in the background."

"Not that. . . ." For a moment a note of exasperation crept into her voice. "You're a long way from being stupid darling. . . ."

"That's better. A moment ago you said I was a fool."

She smiled up at him. "Oh, I don't suppose I shall get anywhere with you, but you know exactly what I mean."

"You mean I'm in the doghouse because somebody took a potshot at me. It's only a very minor flesh wound."

"That's not the point. Don't you understand you could have been killed?"

"That could happen whilst I was crossing a road."

She sighed exasperatedly. "What does the doctor say about the arm?"

"I'm supposed to be getting into bed."

She was immediately contrite. Tenderly, as though dealing with a baby, she undressed him, slipping the jacket from round the shoulder on the wounded side and pulling it off the good arm. The shirt had been ripped apart and—something Masters was pleased about—the blood-stained sleeve discarded, so that the worst of the mess was not apparent to her.

He was sitting on the bed in his pants when the sister arrived, carrying a hospital back-tie shirt. She regarded him for a moment. "I think it would be better to get into bed like that Mr Masters, rather than try to inveigle that arm into this."

"Thank heaven for that, Sister. I've never fancied myself in one of those rigouts."

She glanced at Wanda. "I can understand why, can't

you, Mrs Masters? But of course you can." She turned back to Masters. "Right, you Gorgeous Beast, in you get. The doctor will be here shortly. Now, perhaps you can tell me what injections you have already been given. Tetanus? Good. What pain killer? Would it have been pethidine by any chance? Oh, I can see it was. Somebody has very thoughtfully written a label for your jacket. A hundred mils." She adjusted the backrest and pillows behind him. "Now, Mrs Masters, he's going to be perfectly all right, so I think you should go. You can wait if you like, but it will probably be an hour or so. . . ."

"We live just behind the hospital, Sister. It was very thoughtful of somebody to have him brought to the Westminster. If you will tell me when I can come back. . . ."

They were gathered in Masters' office at the Yard, awaiting a call from the Commissioner, when Anderson came in. He shook hands with Pollock, Gudgeon and Moller and then turned to Green. "I've not been in on this caper, as you know, Bill. But I understand that whatever it was you had to do you've done it and covered yourselves in glory. All of you. It's a pity George can't be here, but I understand he's doing pretty well and should be going home in a couple of days. He's to slip into the Westminster each day for a dressing, but he's been given three weeks' convalescent leave to cover that, and he'll get a few days ordinary leave on top."

"I'll believe that when he's had it, sir."

"What? Oh, quite. We seem to rely on him a bit too much. Now, what I really came down about is to tell you that we are to make our way up to Conference Room A and the Commissioner will join us there. He's expecting a report from you, Bill, and from Mr Pollock and he's invited me to be present. So make sure you give an idiot's guide."

"A full report?" demanded Green.

"No. All the first part is covered by a written report from Mr Pollock. I haven't been allowed to read it, but the Commissioner was pleased with it."

"Thanks," said Pollock.

"There will be some questions arising out of it, no doubt. But then we shall want just the last rumbustious bit from you, Bill, because nobody is quite clear about that part. Now, shall we go up, gentlemen?"

When the Commissioner joined them, Green introduced him to Gudgeon and Moller, the only two of the party he had not met previously. The Commissioner said to Pollock: "George Masters has told me how valuable you were to him, Mr Pollock. He said the best thing he did was to ask you to act as moderator over your meetings. In fact he was so impressed by your performance that he has suggested that such a form of control of evidence should be regarded as normal in cases like this. And I must say I was impressed by your report. I shall, of course, tell your Chief Constable of the great contribution you made to the successful outcome of Hosepipe, even though I can tell him nothing of the matters that were dealt with."

"Thank you, sir. May I, in my turn say how great an experience it has been to work with your officers under George Masters' guidance. This is the second time I've collaborated with them, and I hope it won't be the last."

"That's what I like to hear," said the Commissioner. "Now, gentlemen, if you will sit at the table, I'd like to know about the last act in the drama."

After they were seated, he continued. "I referred to this business as a drama, because it appears to me to have become a drama—literally. George Masters actually wrote the script. He reported to me towards the end of last week. Between that time and the incident in the Bank of Cyrenaica on Tuesday, he wrote a press release and a brief for the Home Secretary as a basis for a statement in the House. Very little of what he wrote had to be altered. And this was before the event. I had those two manuscripts in my hands early on Tuesday morning, with a covering letter from Masters asking me—directing me—to edit them according to how the business turned out.

"I admired what I gathered Masters' plan to be. But the details were not there, and I had to guess what he was about. Quite frankly, gentlemen, I didn't like my thoughts. I smelt danger, but I was in no position to intervene as the show was entirely Masters'. But such uncanny prescience has me bemused. I didn't believe any officer could foresee so nearly what was to happen. I have been proved wrong. Mr Green, please tell me how DCS Masters and, indeed, all of you, worked the business out."

Green cleared his throat.

"Sir, the plan that went into operation was entirely the work of George Masters, and came about as the result of the chin-wag he had with you.

"We had all arrived at the conclusion that to get Hopcraft out of that Bank without spilling the beans was well-nigh impossible, and we reckoned that whatever we did would be dangerous for Hopcraft. We wouldn't have put it past those people to put a bullet in him to stop us getting him alive.

"We reckoned that we either had to fool them into moving Hopcraft, in which case we could have got him in the open or that we had, in some way, to knock out the people in the bank. We toyed with ideas like putting knock-out drops in their milk to achieve this.

"George obviously disliked all of these ideas. But what you've got to remember, sir, is that George is a copper first and foremost, and the idea of breaking the law for whatever reason doesn't come easy for him. However, you told him that the job had to be done, that secrecy had to be maintained and that he was on his own as far as official backing was concerned.

"So George thought it over. He reckoned that to preserve secrecy, he would have to camouflage whatever way of extracting Hopcraft he decided on. From there he went on to realize that a bank-raid would be generally accepted as the work of villains, not of police. That would go some way towards keeping our name out of it. So he thought up a bogus whisper about a raid at some unknown bank. That opened the thing up a bit, because it allowed armed police to be on the spot in any bank without causing too much surprise. So he was still preserving secrecy.

"Then he reckoned he needed a lure. By that, I mean something pretty dramatic to get a reaction out of the bank staff. He cast himself as the lure, knowing that he could well be facing a gun before he'd been inside the bank for more than a minute. But he thought the gun would be in the hands of that bloke Juri. George had asked to see him, to get him to the counter. He used the forged notes business as an excuse to get him there. George had shown his identity, so Juri knew just who he was, and George also knew Juri would have seen him through the security cameras. So he expected Juri to come prepared for trouble."

"Why?" demanded the Commissioner.

"Because he reckoned that any man holding an important hostage would be uptight if a senior cop appeared on the premises. George had said he wanted to talk about forged notes, but he'd purposely asked for Juri by name. He didn't just bowl in and ask the cashier who he should talk to about forged currency. A bit of a giveaway, George thought, but it was a risk he had to take and so he expected Juri would be very much on the alert and prepared for trouble."

"Thank you."

Green continued.

"George intended, as soon as Juri appeared, to ask straight out to see Dr Hopcraft. He expected to get a reaction if Juri believed the meeting was to be genuinely about forged notes. Fear, a flicker of the eyes, a pause before replying . . . you know what I mean. But in any case, George had armed himself with a bogus warrant to search the premises. He would have produced it if necessary and that would have caused a reaction. But he had expected Juri to draw a gun on him, and that would have given him an excuse to do whatever he wanted. That's why he purposely went in unarmed, so

that nobody could accuse him of having started anything. But he'd taken the precaution of having three of
us go in there with him, all armed. And he'd left DCS
Pollock, Sergeant Berger and Dr Moller outside. Their
job was to head off any police interference if outside
alarm bells started to ring. We were to shut the bank
door and the DCS and the sergeant were to tell any police officers who came roaring up that DCS Masters was
inside and had everything under control. He'd gone in
with a team to foil a raid. Mr Pollock's seniority would
have accomplished that.

"George reckoned he had the secrecy buttoned up,
whatever happened. He sussed that he could blackmail
those Libyans into keeping quiet or he'd bung them all
inside for kidnapping. As it happens, that ploy worked.
But things didn't go quite according to plan. George had
expected that Hopcraft might be guarded, but he hadn't
expected two London villains to be on the premises, nor
that they'd lose their heads and come out shooting. As I
said, he thought Juri might produce a gun and threaten
him, but with three of us there in the bank, not with
him, exactly, but pretending to be customers and all
armed, he reckoned that side could be safely taken care
of.

"We had, of course, spent days watching the bank to
see when it was likely to be empty of other customers,
and we were lucky enough to find a moment when it
was empty. Easy enough, really, because I don't think
it's got many ordinary customers coming in to cash
cheques and what not. But for all George's planning, the
reaction came from those villains, Farries and Crease,
who had obviously been warned by Juri. They misread
the situation. They thought George was alone and unarmed. The silly bastards opened up on him. He was
hit, as you know. The three of us returned the fire. Naturally, we shot to kill, so Farries and Crease died. We
fired two shots each.

"And that was that, really sir. No external alarm had
been set ringing, but we closed the door and started to

search the building. George had the plans, so we knew what we were about. We rounded up the senior staff, got the keys and released Hopcraft, who'd been living and working down below. George was in pain, but he was fit enough to put the fear of Allah up those characters. He didn't take long about it, either. And Mr Pollock left them in no doubt as to what he'd do if they contradicted a single word of the plan George had written up. Farries and Crease were bank robbers. We'd foiled the raid and shot them dead in the process. That was George's cover story. By the time an ambulance and a quack arrived, everything had been seen to. Hopcraft was fit enough to come out with us. We said he was a customer in the bank but he hadn't seen anything because he had been doing a bit of business with an under-manager in an upstairs office. So nobody even wanted to know his name. I got you on the blower from the bank, sir, and George had a word with you about the press release. You know the rest."

"Thank you very much, Green," said the Commissioner. "It was much as I expected, but I take my hat off to Masters, not only for putting himself up like a clay pigeon to be shot at, but for all the bits and pieces he added to make the thing sound authentic. Repatriation of currency! How in hell's name did he think that one up!"

"It happens, sir," said Green.

"Does it? Really?"

Green nodded. "It would have been unsafe to use something that doesn't take place."

"I see. Well, now, Mr Pollock, there are just one or two things. . . ."

". . . and why couldn't the police have arrested the two men before they entered the bank? The police must have known of the raid, otherwise why were they armed? The Minister owes the House a full explanation of how this deplorable killing came to happen in this city and on the premises of a foreign state."

The opposition questioner sat down and the Home Secretary rose.

"Mr Speaker, in anticipation both of this question and the source whence it came, I have prepared a statement concerning the events which took place in the Bank of Cyrenaica at lunchtime on Tuesday.

"I feel sure there are many members who would wish to hear the full facts of the matter and so I would ask the House to bear with me if my reply is as detailed as the Honourable Member opposite has asked."

The Home Secretary lowered the paper supplied by Masters in advance of the raid.

"Members will appreciate that these days much use is made of bank notes of high denominations—din shops, pay packets, rail booking-offices and such like places."

"The price of inflation," said a voice. The Minister ignored it.

"I refer, in this instance, mainly to the twenty- and fifty-pound notes which are now commonplace. Notes of such high values naturally attract the attention of forgers. They are worth making, in fact.

"Some months ago, in the early days of last September, to be more precise, it became obvious to us that small numbers of forged notes of these denominations were being fed into the system. They were particularly good forgeries, and it took a practised eye to detect them. Naturally, we had to take immediate action to stem the inflow of counterfeit currency and, indeed, to employ the best possible team from within our police forces to track down the source, to arrest the manufacturers and to confiscate their equipment.

"You will all have heard that Detective Chief Superintendent Masters was wounded on Tuesday."

Rumbles of sympathy from members.

"Mr Masters was leading the investigating team which was made up of several policemen and experts of his own choosing. Mr Masters is probably better known—indeed he is famous—as an investigator of murders, in which field he has shown such great acumen and achieved so much success, that he was a man very suitable to be chosen to lead the investigation of the forgery problem.

"Some days ago, whilst painstakingly tracing some of the counterfeit currency back to source, Mr Masters discovered that some of these notes had been passed by a Mr Juri, a Libyan in the employ of the Bank of Cyrenaica, in payment for a holiday cottage down in the west country. Mr Juri had very kindly offered to pay quite a large sum in notes rather than embarrass the owner of the property by offering a cheque on his own bank. Apparently the Cyrenaican cheques, being uncommon and therefore not generally recognized by the public, are not quite so acceptable as is cash to seaside landladies."

Ripple of laughter.

"Mr Masters was, by this time, coming to the conclusion that much of the counterfeit money was being put into circulation through foreign banks, where the employees are not so familiar with our bank notes and are, therefore, less likely to recognize a forgery. So, last Tuesday, armed with nothing more than an envelope containing the bad notes, Mr Masters called at the bank to speak to Mr Juri, in an effort to discover if Mr Juri could provide any information as to how they had come to be in his possession."

The Home Secretary paused and then took up the brief he had formerly put on the despatch box.

"At this point I must diverge a little. As every member of this House must be aware, the police forces of this country rely heavily on what are known as whispers. A whisper from this source that a hijacking is to take place, a whisper from another source that a burglary is intended. And so on. Mr Speaker, you will realize that each of these whispers has to be tested and weighed, for some are more reliable than others and the less reliable, if not judged to be so, could waste a lot of police time and public money.

"The Metropolitan Police had heard such a whisper.

One that merely informed them that there was to be a bank raid in London on Tuesday. The source was a reliable one, but the information was incomplete. No hint of the bank to be robbed, the time, or even those involved was forthcoming. But, as I said, the source was a reliable one and so, even though lacking in detail, the whisper could not be ignored. Because of this, last Tuesday, there was a limited issue of arms, and small squads of armed policemen, were scattered about the capital, in vehicles, doing their normal patrolling, but ready to rush to any spot at the first hint of trouble.

"As Detective Superintendent Masters had his team out and about in the business areas where he was proposing to call on a number of banks—one of them the Bank of Cyrenaica—it was felt that this team, too, could be one of those prepared to assist, should there be a raid in the area where they were conducting enquiries. To this end, three revolvers were issued to the team. I wish to stress that the two Detective Superintendents, Masters and Pollock were not armed.

"Masters entered the Bank of Cyrenaica with two other policemen, both armed. They were not anticipating what happened. DCS Masters approached the counter and stated his business to an employee, who proceeded to use the internal phone to tell Mr Juri that a senior police officer had called and would like to speak to him. Mr Juri asked the employee if DCS Masters was at liberty to say what was the purpose of the interview. Masters, quite openly stated that it concerned forged bank notes. That was as far as he had got when an internal door in the bank slammed open and two armed men appeared. It seems they had, somehow, penetrated into the back quarters of the bank and that somebody there had set an alarm bell ringing. The bank is fitted with security cameras and it is thought that somehow the two armed men had caught sight of DCS Masters and his companions, had recognized them as policemen, and had jumped to the conclusion that they had arrived to foil the raid on which the two were engaged. They both opened fire. The first shot wounded DCS Masters who was, as I have already observed, unarmed. His two companions, who were standing back from the counter, chatting, were as much taken by surprise as Masters, but within a moment or two they had drawn their weapons and were firing back.

"On such occasions, the police are under instructions to shoot to kill, and both the officers supporting Mr Masters were trained marksmen, because weapons are never issued to other than trained shots. Both officers had been issued with six bullets. Both returned four with their weapons after the affair. So far, seven rounds fired from the weapons of the two robbers have been found. Mercifully, none of the bank staff was hurt—they had been trained to fall to the ground in such an emergency and they had promptly taken that precaution. Another man in the bank—a customer—was unhurt and rendered the police all the assistance in his power which was, I believe, to help the wounded Chief Superintendent.

"Mr Speaker, I have described these events at some length so as to prevent misunderstanding of the action taken by a number of gallant men. Perhaps I should also add, that it is now felt that we know the purpose of the foiled raid. Members may or may not have heard of a custom called the repatriation of currency. Quite simply this means that each country gathers together at some central bank the currencies of other countries, to return them for credit and recirculation. Last Tuesday was such a day. Libya was returning to this country a large bundle of Sterling notes. These were to go to the Bank of Cyrenaica from where they would be returned to the Bank of England or used in other appropriate ways. All the notes would be used ones, and so most attractive to bank robbers, who naturally fight shy of new notes whose numbers can be traced. It is believed the two men knew of this repatriation which, unfortunately, is often carried out in a less secure manner than is prudent in these days. Exactly what their plans were, the police have been unable to ascertain, since both are dead and their companion in the getaway car has not yet been apprehended.

"Mr Speaker, I have taken the unusual step of describing this incident in some detail, and I must thank the House for hearing me out so patiently. But as it has been said in some quarters that the police were aware of the intentions of the robbers and deliberately allowed them to proceed with their crime in order to provide the opportunity for gunning them down, I felt that the record should be put straight. Had the police known what was to happen, the bank would have been cleared, road-blocks set up, rifles issued—as they are more accurate than revolvers—and DCS Masters would not have deliberately entered a hornet's nest unarmed. As it is, we must be truly thankful the robbers were not armed with sawn-off shotguns and that DCS Masters was not wounded even more severely."

The Home Secretary sat down amid murmurs of appreciation for his account and for the good work of the police.

Pollock had been asked to give a TV interview:

"This counterfeiting of notes affects all areas of the country, so it is not the business of just one force. For some time now there has been provision made for officers from different forces to co-operate in investigating crime that crosses force boundaries. I was helping DCS Masters with the problem, and that's why I was at the bank with him when the raid took place."

"I think we all now understand that, Mr Pollock. You and your colleagues foiled the bank raid, but what about the counterfeiting problem which was your primary task?"

"I can't give you details, obviously, because the matter is *sub judice*, but we have discovered the presses, the plates, the paper and a great number of counterfeit notes."

"That is good to hear. But what about the counterfeiters themselves? Did you catch them?"

"Unfortunately, we didn't. We expected to and we reckon we would have done if this bank raid hadn't cropped up and blown our cover. We were working secretly, of course, but reports of the raid got out and the couterfeiters fled. Within minutes, perhaps. The indications are they've gone overseas. Before we could get to them, they'd . . ."

"Thank you very much, Mr Pollock. We shall have to stop you there, in the knowledge that there won't, after all, be a flood of counterfeit notes in our shops and banks."

"Charles," said Wanda to Gudgeon, "I really haven't had time to thank you properly for moving out to make room for Doris, but she really has been a great help in looking after Michael while I've been going to the hospital several times a day."

"Think nothing of it, my dear. I've done very well with Bill Green and Fred Pollock. Besides, I couldn't have stayed with George away."

"You . . . ? Oh, I see. I suppose not. Husband in hospital and strange man in the house. That wouldn't do, would it?"

"No. How is the old boy?"

"I'm just going over to fetch him home."

"Anything I can do?"

"Not unless you'd like to wait to see him."

"Not today. I believe Pollock and I will be coming round tomorrow to say goodbye. He's giving me a lift home, you know. But about the cottage. You're to come when you want to, and I wouldn't be at all surprised if we can't let the three of you have my cottage all to yourselves for a fortnight."

"We, Charles?"

"It appears that Mrs Lawson and I both have designs on each other. We're thinking of doing something about it sooner rather than later, so we shall only need the one cottage between us."

"Marriage, Charles?"

"The real thing, my dear. I wouldn't want anything else."

"Congratulations. I'm looking forward to meeting Mrs Lawson."

"She'll probably be Mrs Gudgeon by then, but I must confess that I want her to meet you. And George, of course. I think Beryl will value your friendship as much as I do."

"What a nice thing to say, Charles."

"It was meant to be, my dear. I knew when George put me away years ago that he fought for me, though I wouldn't pay heed to him at the time. Since meeting him again and working with him . . . well, he's my type of man."

"Did you say George put you away?"

"Arrested me."

"What for?"

"Killing one of the men who killed my wife."

"The other got away?"

Gudgeon shook his head. "No, my dear. George gave him to me on a plate. His name was Farries."

"The one who . . . ?"

"The same. Now that account is squared I can go to Beryl Lawson with a clear conscience, even though I am an ex-con."

"And George led you to him?"

"Not quite. George recruited me and Farries happened along."

"I suspect you saved George's life."

"If I did, I am happy to have done it. He's a lucky man who can kill two birds with one stone."

Wanda said: "George, did you know that Farries would be in that bank for Charles to shoot at him?"

"No, poppet."

"Did you know Farries was connected with the case?"

"There was a hint that he might be, in so far as his boss, Crease, was seen speaking to Juri four or five months ago."

"Is that all?"

"Yes. Darling, why this catechism?"

"Charles thinks you handed Farries to him on a plate."

"Oh, does he! Then he's wrong. Bill Green and I have been bursting a gut to prevent Charles getting to hear that there was the slightest chance of Farries being involved."

"Because you knew what he might do?"

Masters looked at her. "Because I knew he loved his wife, my precious one. As I love mine. And I wouldn't care to think what my reactions might be were a villain to harm her." He put his good arm round her. "But that's enough of that, except to say that I owe Charles, Bill and Sergeant Reed a debt of gratitude. I suggest we now drop the subject and. . . ."

"And what?"

He grinned. "I suppose about all I'm good for with one arm in a sling is to join you in a cup of tea."

She smiled at him.

"Don't they say a shot in the arm works wonders for the recipient? As a stimulant, I mean. If so. . . ."

There's an epidemic with 27 million victims. And no visible symptoms.

It's an epidemic of people who can't read.

Believe it or not, 27 million Americans are functionally illiterate, about one adult in five.

The solution to this problem is you... when you join the fight against illiteracy. So call the Coalition for Literacy at toll-free **1-800-228-8813** and volunteer.

**Volunteer
Against Illiteracy.
The only degree you need
is a degree of caring.**

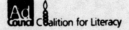